Published 2018 by Timberdoodle Press.

E-Book ISBN# 978-1-945856-03-7

Print Book ISBN# 978-1-945856-38-9

Cover Art courtesy dreamtime.com and depositphoto.com

Author's note:

The title *Slow Walk* is derived from a hunting technique commonly known as "still hunting." When a hunter "still hunts" he moves very, very slowly through the forest, often waiting several minutes between each step. As you can imagine, it takes a great deal of focus and patience.

I believe finding one's way in a strange, post-apocalyptic world would require moving forward very slowly, much as a still hunter does. Where to get food? Shelter? Clothing? Medicine? Who to trust?

In my imagined post-upheaval world none of the necessities of life can be purchased at a store. Hospitals no longer exist. Imagine trying to survive under those conditions. The challenges would be enormous.

Thinking about the difficulties and how different personalities would react to them led me to write the Upheaval series.

SLOW WALK

THE UPHEAVAL BOOK 1

CHARLEY MARSH

TIMBERDOODLE PRESS

1

SYDNEY DID her best thinking in her grandfather's musty old hay loft. She lay on her stomach atop a pile of loose hay she had raked together and gazed out through the hay door. The post and beam barn soared three stories high, giving her a view of the entire farm.

In the distance she caught a sliver of light dancing off the Mississippi River. Thunderheads gathered in the west. She could already smell the rain they carried.

The hay loft had always been one of Sydney's favorite spots on the farm to get away and be alone. She rolled onto her back and watched the dust float through the shafts of sunlight that penetrated between the shrunken barn boards. Pigeons cooed and strutted on the highest crossbeams overhead.

Her grandfather, called Pops by everyone who knew him, was getting worse; she could no longer deny it. His dementia had reared its insidious head four months ago. At first it made Sydney and her sister laugh. He did foolish, forgetful things that she and Shannon shook their heads at and promptly forgot about.

The laughter ended last night when Pops almost succeeded in burning down the house. The clang of pots from the kitchen had woken Sydney a little after midnight. She assumed her grandfather was warming milk—a favorite of his when his heartburn acted up. When she heard the front door slam she crawled out of bed to investigate and found the wood stove roaring, doors wide open with hot embers popping and snapping onto the floor.

She shouted for Shannon, closed the stove, and poured water over the burning hot spots. Shannon carried the smoking hearth rug outside and dumped it into the rain barrel at the corner of the house. They found Pops shuffling in a circle partway down the long drive, disoriented and belligerent. He had no idea who they were and it took two hours of cajoling to convince him to return to the house and his bed.

Pops needed round-the-clock watching now, Sydney realized. It was going to be difficult with only the two of them, but somehow she and Shannon would work it out. They could take turns sleeping on the floor in front of Pop's bedroom door; if he took another walk in the middle of the night he'd wake his watcher.

Satisfied with the solution, Sydney allowed her eyes to close. The old hay smelled sweet and made a soft bed. She decided she had time for a short nap while Shannon watched over Pops. She'd rest for a bit, then relieve her twin sister.

———

At first Sydney thought the screams were part of her dream. Her eyes fluttered open and then closed again. She wasn't ready to wake up, it had been a long night with her grandfather.

Another scream pierced the air. She rolled to her knees and looked toward the house. A man stood in the open door, another on the step below him.

Desperate Ones. Survivors of the great upheavals that had changed the face of the earth and wiped out most of mankind. People unable or too lazy to fend for themselves, they chose instead to forcibly take from others. The first had arrived at her family's farm a little more than a year ago. It had taken them two years to pillage their way from the east coast and across the Mississippi River.

Sydney and her sister and grandfather had been happy at first to share what little they had, but as the waves of refugees kept coming it dawned on them that they themselves would not survive if they continued to feed everyone who wandered by their farm.

The trio did their best to feed the children, but they informed the adults that it was time they learned to fend for themselves. Most of the people accepted this with resignation, grateful that at least the children were fed.

Some people did not. They became predators, willing to harm others in order to get what they wanted. Sydney named the predators 'The Desperate Ones.'

Icy fear washed over Sydney as two men dragged Shannon from the house. Her sister bucked and jerked in their hands, trying to escape. Afraid the men would spot her, Sydney pressed her body flat on the loft floor and tried to think of a way to help her sister. Two of the men held Shannon's arms while a third removed her pants and covered her with his body.

Bile rose in Sydney's throat. She tried to choke it back but couldn't. She twisted to the side and vomited. A clammy sweat broke out on her skin and she began to shake. She covered her ears, trying to block out the sound of the men's laughter mixed with Shannon's screams.

Sydney's weapons lay hidden under her bed with no way to get into the house and retrieve them without being seen. She would end up like Shannon if she tried. She cursed her cowardice, told herself that her twin was strong; the rape was horrible, but her sister would survive and eventually get over it.

Another man took his place between Shannon's legs. Shannon tore an arm free and raked her long nails down the rapist's cheek.

Sydney saw blood glisten and drip down the side of the man's face. *Good for her.* Shannon had always been the tougher and braver of the two. Her curiosity and fearless nature made her a born leader and were traits that Sydney lacked.

Sydney's satisfaction was short-lived. The man roared in anger and slammed Shannon's face with his fist, then grabbed her head and twisted. Shannon lay still beneath him.

"Jesus, Sandman, what'd you have to go and do that for? I didn't get my turn. Besides, Pharaoh woulda paid us good money for a beauty like her."

The man called Sandman got to his feet and gave Shannon a vicious kick. "The bitch cut me. Forget her. Let's see if there's anything worth taking in the house and get out of here."

Sydney couldn't catch her breath. She inched forward and looked down at her sister's limp body, willing her to move. *Come on, Shannon. You can't die on me, I need you.* A whimper escaped her throat and she buried it against the back of her hand.

Her sister's killer came out of the house and looked toward the barn.

Too late, Sydney realized he would see her if he looked up to the hay loft. She ducked back from the loft door and prayed he hadn't noticed.

"Hey, I just saw something move in that barn," said Sandman. "Abel, come with me." The two men strode across the yard toward the barn.

2

OH CRAP. Crap, crap, crap. They're going to find me. Sydney looked around the empty loft in a desperate panic. There was no place to hide. A cooing pigeon caught her attention and gave her an idea. She pulled off her teeshirt and tiptoed under the pigeons, then waved her arms at them, flapping the tee against the beams. The flock of birds took off in a noisy whir of wings and flew out the hay loft door.

"Bah. It's just pigeons," said Abel. "I already checked inside there. The barn's empty, nothing worth taking. Let's grab the food and get out of here. The old man ain't going to stop us, he's crazy in the head."

The voices receded. Sydney put her tee back on and quietly stepped back to the loft door, careful to keep out of sight. The one they called Sandman hollered to the two inside the house. One came out carrying a sack that Sydney assumed was filled with her family's food.

The fourth man, short and skinny with long, matted black hair, ran out the door cackling with glee. "Let's go. I set a fire in the kitchen. It'll take care of the witness—the old guy's too out of it to know enough to leave."

Sandman stared at the fourth man for a moment, then shook his head. "There ain't no law around here, Bug. Who's the old guy gonna tell? The fire could draw someone's attention. You don't have the brains you were born with, you know that?"

The four men set off down the farm's drive, Bug in the rear. Sydney watched as he turned to look at the flames licking up the outside back corner of the house and pumped his fist in the air. She wondered if Bug was short for firebug.

As soon as the men were out of sight, Sydney climbed down from the loft and ran to the house. She stopped by Shannon's body to check for a pulse, but it was obvious from her sister's open, glazed eyes that she was dead. Sydney shook off the searing pain that tore through her chest. There would be time enough to deal with Shannon later. She had to save her grandfather first.

"Pops! Pops! Where are you?" Sydney ran into the house and headed for her grandfather's bedroom. She found him sitting by the west-facing window, the ironwood staff/walking stick she had carved for his previous birthday across his lap.

In memory of her grandfather's sheep farm, the figure of a ram's head, horns elegantly curled, topped the staff. Famous across the midwest and western mountains for the care and quality of his breeding program, the sheep had been her grandfather's lifelong passion.

Pops turned his head from the window and looked at Sydney while he fingered the ram's head carving. "There you are, Gabriella. There's a thunderstorm moving in. We need to bale the hay I cut two days ago before it gets rained on."

Sydney swallowed the painful lump in her throat. Gabriella was her mother, a talented artist who had died when the first tsunamis hit the East coast. A major New York

City art gallery had sponsored a one-woman show of her mother's work and paid for her to attend the show's opening night party. Her mother had been so excited by the acknowledgement of her talent. Unfortunately, none of the family had been able to go with her to New York.

Their father, a wildlife biologist, had flown to Yellowstone that weekend to join a group of scientists studying the effects of the earthquakes that were hitting the park more and more frequently.

Shannon and Sydney had volunteered to stay with their grandfather and help with the spring lambing, a job the whole family usually participated in. Three long years had passed since the girls had last seen their parents.

Sydney shook off the memories. There was no time for them now, she needed to focus on the current crisis. She heard the fire crackle and watched as tendrils of gray smoke began to curl along the ceiling of her grandfather's bedroom. A shelf of plates in the kitchen hit the floor with a crash. The fire was gaining momentum.

"Pops, we have to check the baler first. I can't get it to feed the baling twine properly and I need your help." Sydney kept her tone calm while she plucked the ironwood staff from her grandfather's lap and grasped one of his hands to pull him to his feet.

"I don't know why the good Lord didn't see fit to give me sons," grumbled her grandfather. He took the staff from Sydney's hand. "Give me that." He stumped out of the bedroom, oblivious to the gathering smoke.

Sydney resisted the urge to race from the house. She fought the panic that waited to overwhelm her if she gave in to it. Her beloved sister Shannon, her best friend, had been raped and murdered. Shannon had been the one who held the three of them together, the one who figured out how to survive. They would be lost without her.

Sydney couldn't bear the loss of another loved one. Part of her wanted to give up the struggle and let the fire take her so she could join her parents and sister in oblivion.

Instead, she forced herself to walk calmly behind her grandfather and play the part of Gabriella. "We need to hurry, Pops. The rain will be here soon." They stepped outside the house. Behind them the fire began to roar. Sydney took her grandfather's arm and led him away from the house.

Dazed confusion filled her grandfather's face as they walked by Shannon. His eyes darted to her sister's body and away. "Who is that?" He looked at Sydney's almost identical face. "Who are you? Where's Gabriella?"

"Gabriella's gone, Pops. I'm your granddaughter, Sydney, remember?" But he didn't remember, and she wondered if he would ever know her again. She led him to the glider swing in the side yard, away from the smoke, and left him gently rocking there.

With her grandfather settled, Sydney ran back into the house and grabbed a blanket to wrap her sister's body in. She spread it on the ground beside Shannon, then leaned over to gently close her sister's hazel eyes, so much like their mother's. Sydney's eyes were a soft jade green like her father's. Both girls had inherited their mother's curly black hair and olive skin.

Sydney crossed Shannon's arms and pulled her splayed legs together, then rolled her in the blanket and dragged it to her mother's vegetable garden. She needed to bury the body before the scavengers arrived and she knew the digging would be easiest here.

It took her three hours to dig a hole long enough and

deep enough to hold her sister's body. The rainstorm that had been gathering in the west blew in while she dug, dropping sheets of water over the house and yard and turning the garden to mud.

Sydney moved her grandfather to the barn to keep him dry and returned to her task. She managed to hold her tears at bay until she tamped down the loose earth over Shannon and covered the grave with rocks to keep the scavengers from digging her up. She laid the last rock and stared blindly at the grave, unable to take in the loss of her sister.

A low sob tore loose from the depths of her being. She threw her body beside the grave and wept until she was empty and the rain mixed with her tears.

3

6 MONTHS later

Sydney glided three long steps and stilled in the way of all prey animals: body frozen in the vain hope that a hunter will not see it. She strained to detect the faintest foreign sound. Moving only her eyes, she slowly scanned the spaces between the oaks, hickories and prickly ash that dominated the area, but she saw nothing that alarmed her.

Why then, was her mind on full alert? She spread her awareness out through the trees and shrubs, straining to pick up the tiniest change. She knew this area like she knew her own body: every rock, every tree, every animal den or nest, the patches of wildflowers and the gullies.

This was her land, a place where she felt safe and comfortable, but at this moment it felt alien. She frowned as she tried to pinpoint the source of her wariness.

The forest was too quiet.

That was it—a heavy silence pressed on her ears. No birds sang or twittered in the brush, not even a light breeze rustled the leafy treetops overhead. The unnatural quiet made her feel nervous and afraid.

The local wildlife was used to Sydney's presence. Only minutes ago the upper forest had been filled with the chatter and movement of red squirrels and bluejays grousing at her as she passed through their neighborhoods. Their silence was better than any alarm; it meant that a predator was nearby.

These days the hunter could be man or beast. Either one, Sydney fell onto the prey side of the equation. A thin sheen of sweat broke out on her forehead and back as her fear increased.

She closed her eyes to focus on her other senses. Took a long, deep breath to slow her heartbeat. She smelled earth dampened from a recent rain shower, the rotting leaves of fall, and the sweet ripeness of a large blackberry patch off to her left.

She emptied her mind and listened for several minutes longer, but she heard nothing that shouldn't be there.

She took three more slow steps and again carefully scanned her surroundings. It was an excruciatingly slow, oh so slow, method of movement, but also the safest. Movement is what catches the eye—all eyes—but especially the predator's eye. Movement betrays the predator's quarry.

"Grandmother called it Slow Walking, Syd." She could hear her friend Smokey's voice in her ear, low and gruff. *"The best hunters use it to move undetected through the forest. It takes great patience to execute and is very difficult to master. Few men excel at it. I myself am merely good, but I believe that you have what it takes to be great."*

That had been the summer before her parent's death. It was the last thing Smokey had taught her before he returned home to care for his grandmother with a promise to return the following summer. Six months after Smokey's departure massive earthquakes and tsunamis had wreaked havoc with the planet.

There!

Sydney slowly shifted her eyes toward the sound, careful not to move any other part of her body. She waited. A branch cracked to her right and she heard a large body stumble and then swear.

A man. She fought the urge to run. Running gave away a prey's location. She took three quick but silent steps away from the sound instead, into a nearby stand of prickly ash, ignoring the sharp thorns that ripped against her bare arms and snagged her clothing. She forced herself to stop and wait, to see what the man would do.

"Jeezus, Barrett, what the hell you doin'? I ain't haulin' your ass outta here if you break an ankle. You hear me?"

The voice came from in front of Sydney.

Two men. A small sob escaped her throat before she could contain it. She knew what the men would do to her if they caught her.

She still couldn't see either man, and she was confident that they had not spotted her, but they were much too close for her safety. She needed to slink away without alerting the men to her presence.

Be the fox, not the rabbit, she told herself.

Her slim body trembled with the effort of forcing herself to remain motionless when every cell in her body urged her to RUN! She needed to move carefully, to be sure she moved in the opposite direction from the men and didn't flee into their arms.

She could hear the man to her right, the one called Barrett, swearing softly to himself as he moved away from Sydney. That was good. She breathed a little easier. She turned her attention back to the man in front of her. He was still moving toward her.

Sydney spun around and headed away from the man, placing her feet carefully so she wouldn't break a stick or disturb the forest floor. Leave no trace. When she judged that she had moved a safe distance, she stopped and listened again.

Hunters wait for a prey animal to panic and run. Running was a mistake that meant discovery often followed by death, while hiding, sometimes even hiding in plain sight, could mean survival. These men were hunting—if she wanted to survive she needed to use her wits and wait them out.

"I know I smelled smoke, Cal," called the man named Barrett. "I think it came from somewhere up there on the ridge."

The men's rough voices sounded loud and offensive to Sydney's ears. They didn't belong in her forest. She cursed herself silently—these men were here because of her.

Her grandfather had been doing poorly this morning. His body was losing its ability to generate heat. She had wrapped him in all their blankets, but he continued to shiver. Even though she knew it was only safe to build a fire at night, Sydney had risked a small one for her grandfather. She placed her grandfather's chair next to the fire before leaving to hunt up a squirrel or rabbit for their dinner.

Now that caring act was putting them both in danger.

The sharp crack of a breaking twig alerted Sydney that the men were on the move again. She sniffed the air, relieved that she could no longer detect any smell of woodsmoke. At least her grandfather had not fed the fire; the smoke would have led these men right to him. The biggest danger now was that the men would stumble upon the trail that led to their cave as they wandered through the forest.

She felt torn as she stood and listened to the men's movements. Should she try to distract them? Perhaps she should lead them away and then lose them in the thick underbrush.

"Barrett! Over here!"

Sydney's head snapped around and a jolt of fear shot through her body. How had the second man gotten so close? She cursed herself for her lapse in attention. That was the sort of carelessness that could get her killed—or worse.

She heard the man called Barrett stumble toward her through the woods on her right. The second man popped out from behind a thick stand of bushes only a few yards from where she stood. So much for her training—Sydney reacted as any frightened prey would—she screamed at the sight and turned to run.

Half-hidden by a bushy black beard and dreadlocks that fell to his shoulders, the man's face did not hold a single scrap of kindness. It was the face of cruelty, of a man who enjoyed inflicting pain for fun. His filthy, ragged shirt exposed long, ropey arms. He carried a club in his hand.

"Well, lookee here what I done found. Barrett! Over here!" The man shouted to his companion as he closed in on Sydney.

Sydney stumbled over a tree root and dropped her crossbow pistol. As she struggled to regain her balance the man lunged at her, caught one foot and brought her to the ground. She winced as one of her knees landed on a rock, but pushed the pain aside as she twisted her body and kicked hard at the hand holding her foot.

The man held fast. He dropped his club and wrapped both hands around her ankle. He twisted her foot hard, a sneer on his face. Sydney cried out in surprise, then clamped her mouth shut. She would not show weakness. Weakness invited death and unspeakable atrocities. She willed herself to be strong.

Dread and fear filled her. She closed her eyes to block out the man's evil face. *Who was she kidding?* It didn't matter how she behaved. Weak or strong, she was now the prisoner of a Desperate One, a predator with no conscience. Cruelty followed by death was unavoidable.

She thought of Shannon and resigned herself to a similar fate. She deserved it. She had not come to her sister's aid when Shannon needed her most. She was a coward. It didn't matter that all her weapons had been inside the house and impossible to get to. It didn't matter that she would have been raped and murdered like her sister.

All that mattered is that she chose to hide instead of finding a way to help the one person she loved more than anyone else. The image of her sister's naked, dead body would be forever burned into her mind.

Sydney struggled to pull her foot loose, but the man tightened his grip on her ankle. His strong fingers dug into her and brought tears to her eyes.

A moment later the one called Barrett stumbled and crashed his way to where his companion held Sydney prisoner. "Oh, ho! Good find, Cal. We ain't had us a woman in quite some time, especially a fine, young 'un like this. She's a little on the skinny side, but who ain't these days?" His rough cackle made Sydney shudder.

"Yessiree, I'm lookin' forward to some fresh poontang."

4

S YDNEY OPENED her eyes and wished that she hadn't.

Barrett was the ugliest human being she had ever seen. One wild blue eye stared at her with hunger; the other eye socket was stitched crudely shut with black thread. His large, bulbous nose was bent off to the side at an unnatural angle. He was filthy dirty and his leer revealed blackened teeth with several gaping holes where more than a few had fallen out.

Both men smelled rancid. Bitter bile rose in Sydney's throat and she suppressed a gag, willing herself not to puke.

"You hold her, Barrett. I found her so I get first goes at her," said Cal as he let go of one ankle and fumbled with his pants.

Sydney fought the panic that threatened to overwhelm her and tried to think. If she could get the men walking she might have a chance of escape. She took a deep breath and forced a tremulous smile.

"I ain't had me a real man in a while neither," she said. She emulated the men's speech pattern, hoping it would make her seem more like one of them.

A picture came into her mind of a couple who had stopped by the farm once. The woman was what her mother called a "sex worker," a woman who serviced men for money. The woman had been pretty in a hard way, and she talked rough. Sydney channeled the sex worker's mannerisms. She had always had a knack for mimicry.

"Sure would like to do it right, tho, not here on the hard ground. You gents want to come to my place and get cleaned up first? I got food. We could make a party of it."

She pumped enthusiasm into her words and forced herself to give Cal what she hoped was a flirty look. She guessed that he was the leader of the two, the one she needed to convince, and therefor the one from whom she had the most to fear. She hoped that Barrett would follow Cal's lead.

Cal had his pants unbuttoned and was sliding them down his skinny hips. She sensed that the men were not going to go for her ruse, and she realized that she needed to sweeten her offer, needed to dangle something they couldn't refuse.

"I got a little hooch left too," she added slyly. "I might be willin' to share a bit."

That did it. She saw Barrett lick his lips and knew that she had him. She pushed a little more.

"I even got a purty dress I can put on. We'll have a real party." Sydney sighed and put a pleading note in her voice. "It's been so long since I dressed up and partied..."

Cal gave her a hard, calculating look.

Sydney hoped that he was too macho to ever believe that a skinny teenaged girl would try to get the best of him. She gave him a tentative smile and saw him relax. He pulled his pants back up.

"Git up. And don't try any funny bizness. There's two of us and we don't mind killin' when we hafta. Yer dead body will still be warm long enough to pleasure us."

Sydney nodded meekly, fully into her role now. She got to her feet. "Follow me, gennelmen."

Cal stayed close to her side as she led them toward the trail that ran up the side of the bluff.

Her first thought was to escape and outrun them, but she realized that the men would not just let her go, they would hunt her down. They wouldn't let her get away with making fools of them. She was sure that she could elude them, but her grandfather was immobile, and they would likely find him and kill him.

After the rape and murder of her sister, Sydney and her grandfather lived in the few rooms that had survived the fire. Sydney grew jumpy, paranoid about being found by more Desperate Ones. Images of Shannon's rape were never far from her thoughts. They invaded her dreams and caught her at unexpected moments.

Fear became Sydney's constant companion. In her heart she knew that no matter how much time passed, she would never again feel safe in her family home.

The limestone bedrock along the upper Mississippi River was riddled with underground rivers and caves, but very few of them were suitable for habitation. Massive earthquakes had caused many of the caves to collapse in on themselves, leaving giant sinkholes where farms once stood.

Sydney knew she had to get away from the farm and the scene of Shannon's death. Once she made the decision to move, she spent every day searching the land that surrounded the family homestead until she found something she felt she could work with: a shallow sandstone cave near the top of a bluff. The cave was stable and deep enough to protect them from the elements.

It took her countless trips to transport everything she thought they would need to the cave. Rugs to insulate the cold, damp floor, sleeping pads, blankets, her grandfather's chair. She discovered a small wood stove in one of the barns, took it apart and carried it piece by piece to the cave and reassembled it.

She worked hard to make their new home comfortable. She gathered wood for the stove, sawed lengths from fallen trees and stacked it neatly nearby.

Once everything was moved, she collected rocks and walled in three quarters of the entrance. She left a half foot open on the upper edge for smoke to exit and for air flow, counting on the overhanging sandstone to prevent any rain or snow from entering.

She also left a narrow opening to use as an entrance and hung a piece of heavy canvas for a door. When at last she was finished, Sydney stepped back to admire her work. It certainly couldn't be called luxurious, but she hoped that it would shelter them through the approaching months of cold and inclement weather.

Getting her grandfather up to the cave had been the most difficult part of the move. Crippled from a bad fall many years ago, he frequently lost his balance on uneven ground. Only by convincing him that she was his daughter Gabriella, could she get him to agree to the move. It took her an entire day to get him to the cave. Walk a few steps, rest, explain where they were going, repeat.

By the time they arrived at the cave she wasn't sure he would live through the night, but the old man was tough, and he survived the long, steep climb.

———

Sydney reached the base of the bluff and started up the familiar trail with the two men tagging close behind.

"Hold on there—where you takin' us, girlie?" Cal reached out and grabbed Sydney's arm.

"My place is just up this cliff," she answered, her voice light, and pulled her arm away. She didn't have much time left to come up with a plan. Panic overcame her when she realized that the only way that she would survive this ordeal was to either incapacitate or kill both men.

Cold resolution soon followed her panic. Sydney purposely dredged up images of Shannon's lifeless body. If it came down to kill or be killed, she would kill, she told herself. She had failed her sister. She would not fail her grandfather.

Sydney clenched her jaw and marched on.

The land that Sydney called home consisted of steep hill-sides separated by narrow ravines known to the locals as coolies. The coolies spread out into secluded valleys when they reached the river bottoms. One such valley held her grandfather's sheep farm.

The bluffs rose five hundred feet above the valley floor where they then stretched a thousand miles to the west, with little change in elevation until they reached the foothills of the Rocky Mountains in Colorado.

Sydney led the men up the face of one of these steep bluffs. She followed a game trail that zigged and zagged its way up terrain that at times stood nearly vertical. It was tough going, sometimes forcing a climber to hands and knees, but she was in shape for it. She climbed these bluffs every day in her search for food.

The two men were not quite as agile as Sydney, and she had to be careful not to get so far ahead of them that they became alarmed. As she hiked, she worked out a plan. Near the top of the bluff the trail skirted around a large sandstone outcropping and made a sharp turn. The turn presented her first opportunity to attack her captors.

She glanced back to check on Cal and Barrett's progress. They were grasping at trees to help pull themselves up the steep trail. It gave her a small amount of satisfaction to see that both men were red in the face from the effort of keeping up with her pace.

Cal had moved ahead of Barrett. Good. Cal was the smarter of the two men and therefore her greatest danger; she wanted to deal with him first. "C'mon fellas, we're almost there," she called out in a teasing singsong, encouraging them to follow her.

Sydney reached the critical turn a few minutes later. She scooted around the rocky point, squeezed her body into a narrow crevice, and waited for Cal to appear.

The crevice was a tight fit. The sandstone was rough and cold on her arms and it pressed against her shoulders. She made herself stand perfectly still and slowed her breathing while she waited.

The trail narrowed to a mere three feet in width here. On the uphill side stood the sandstone outcrop where Sydney waited in hiding. The downhill side had been sheered off during the quakes when a massive slide tore away a portion of the bluff.

Sydney's plan counted on the fact that the men wouldn't be able to see the drop-off until they rounded the point.

She heard their voices draw closer and held her breath. She would need perfect timing and a lot of luck to catch Cal off guard. She would only get one chance.

An onset of nerves made her shake, and she forced herself to let her breath out and relax. She strained to hear the approaching men over her pounding heart. Who knew that a heartbeat could sound so loud?

A moment later she heard scuffling footsteps nearby. She forced herself to be patient. Breathe. If she moved too soon she would lose the element of surprise and the opportunity to eliminate one of her captors.

5

SYDNEY bent her knees and wedged her shoulders and arms tight against the crevice walls. Another few seconds passed. The front edge of a body came into sight.

She brought her knees up and lashed out with her feet as hard as she could. Her feet connected with the man's hips. Sydney watched, heart thudding in her chest, as he tottered for a moment, then windmilled his arms as he tried to catch his balance. For a moment he hung on the cliff edge and Sydney feared failure. Then he simply disappeared.

She heard a shout followed by a thud when he hit the rocks below, and then silence. Even if he had survived the fall of several hundred feet he would not be in any condition to come after her. One down, one to go.

Sydney slid out of the crevice and turned to run. A hand grabbed her long braid and yanked hard, snapping her head back. She struggled to stay on her feet.

Barrett wrapped the braid around his hand and pulled her against his chest. He hissed in her ear. "Bitch. Cal told you not to try anything funny."

Sydney's heart stopped beating for a moment. She gulped

air and wished she hadn't. Barrett's rank, sour smell made her choke and cough. Her knees wobbled and she stumbled.

Barrett's grip on her hair tightened. He twisted her head around, forcing Sydney to look into his hideous face. His good eye was narrowed and cold with fury. He squeezed her jaw hard with his free hand, his fingers digging into her cheeks.

"I should throw you off this cliff to join Cal, and I just might do that later, but I got bizness with you, girl. When I'm done you'll wish that I had tossed you over first."

Sydney was stunned by the pain of his grip. No one had ever intentionally hurt her before today. She clenched her stomach muscles, blinked back tears, and again willed herself not to show weakness.

Barrett pushed her away from his body, picked up Cal's dropped club, and jabbed her hard in the back.

Sydney gasped. A new fear lodged deep in her belly. It became clear to her that Barrett would not leave her alive once he was finished with her. She was going to end up raped and murdered just like her sister.

"Now git movin' and take me to your home." Barrett jabbed her again, and Sydney stumbled forward. "Any more funny bizness and I'll be only too happy to give you more of this here club. Don't matter to me if I break a few bones before I have my fun. Might even make it more enjoyable."

Sydney knew she couldn't bear to have this filthy, brutal excuse for a man violate her body. For a brief moment she considered leaping over the trail edge and ending her life. Then she remembered her grandfather. Pops was waiting, weak and vulnerable, dependent upon her return. She couldn't leave him to face Barrett alone.

She gathered up her courage and slowly headed up the trail.

They were only a few minutes from Sydney's cave. She tried to come up with a way to delay their arrival, but Barrett kept his eye on her and the club pushed into her back. He was making certain that there would be no opportunities for Sydney to elude him.

She eyed her crossbow out of the corner of her eye. Barrett carried it slung over one shoulder. Maybe she could…no, it would be impossible to snatch it off him.

To her dismay, they arrived at the cave before she could come up with a plan. Sydney eyed the rock wall she had constructed. There was no smoke wafting from the top edge. Pop must have let the fire go out.

A sudden fear that her grandfather's condition had worsened while she was dealing with Cal and Barrett made her quicken her pace.

"No you don't." Barrett grabbed her braid again and held her back. "You stay right next to me while I take a look inside. There'll be no more surprises from you." He pushed aside the piece of canvas that hung over the doorway and peered inside. "Who's the old man?"

"That's my grandfather. Please leave him alone, he's senile and very weak. He couldn't hurt a fly, he can barely move."

Sydney despised the begging tone that crept into her voice, but she was afraid of what Barrett might do to her helpless grandfather. What if he hurt Pop just to punish her for killing Cal? She couldn't bear it if her grandfather suffered because of her.

"Humph. We'll see about that." Barrett pushed through the canvas flap and entered the cave.

Still held by her braid, Sydney had no choice but to follow him. She needed a plan and she needed it fast, but her mind was a blank.

Sydney's eyes adjusted to the dimmer light of the cave as

she watched Barrett move around the small space. She had done her best to make the cave homelike; besides the rugs that covered the dirt floor, she had tucked a couple of small dressers against the rear wall.

There was enough room near the entrance to stand upright and move around, and she only had to bend over slightly at the back of the space.

Her grandfather sat on a folding camp chair near the small wood stove with his bad leg propped up on a box. She started toward him but Barrett pointed his club at her and she stopped. Sydney was learning to heed Barrett's club.

Her grandfather's head was hanging down and she couldn't see his chest rise and fall. Sadness and relief swept through her. At least Pops would escape Barrett's cruelty and he wouldn't witness whatever happened to her. Then she saw the faint rise of his chest and knew that he was still breathing.

"I need to check my grandfather," she said as firmly as she could, and started toward him again.

Barrett blocked her path. "No. Leave him be. What you need to do is fix me some food. Your grandfather will be fine as long as he stays where he is and doesn't try anything foolish. What you got to eat?"

Sydney was still wearing the small backpack that she used when hunting game. She slid it off her back and pulled two dead squirrels from the pack.

"I can prepare these if you let me make a small fire in the stove."

Barrett considered her for a moment and then nodded. "Okay then. But keep in mind that I'm watchin' every move you make. You try anythin' and I'll hurt the old man first, then you. Got that?"

"Yes, I understand. You like to inflict pain," Sydney said.

She didn't try to hide the bitter edge in her voice. Her hands were tied as long as Pops was a hostage. He was all she had left in the world, and she would endure whatever cruelty the monster standing next to her dished out if it meant keeping her grandfather safe.

"I'll need to skin these squirrels. My tools are in the box over there. May I get them?"

Barrett walked over to the box and looked inside. He upended the box and grabbed the sharpest knife from the small pile of tools. He picked up the empty box, set it beside her grandfather and sat on it.

"I'll use this knife on yer grandfather if you don't behave. It'll be very slow and painful, I promise you. Now git workin' on those squirrels."

Sydney glared at Barrett and then pulled a second knife from the pile. She picked up the squirrels and started to leave the cave.

Barrett jumped to his feet and blocked her path. "Whoa, now, where the hell do you think you're goin'?"

"I can't clean them in here, it will attract vermin."

Barrett shook his head and gave her a sinister grin. "Vermin are the least of yer worries, little girl. I'd say you've already attracted the king of vermin. A little joke, eh?" He chuckled, a low, mean sound that ended in a cough.

Gooseflesh rose on Sydney's body and she suppressed a shudder.

"You ain't goin' nowhere, girlie, unnerstand? Work in that back corner where I kin keep my eye on you."

Sydney stood for a moment and looked at Barrett before complying. She understood that he had no intention of leaving her, or her grandfather, alive. He would take what he wanted from them and when he was finished he would kill them both. Barrett was that sort of man: a man who held no respect for the sanctity of life.

The knowledge was like ice water in her veins. She took a deep, shaky breath and moved to the back corner of the cave to clean the squirrels and think. *I need a plan!*

Her mind refused to cooperate. It filled with ugly images of her short future and what Barrett planned to do to her. She tried to push them away but the image of Shannon, broken and naked, persisted.

She swallowed a small sob before it could escape her lips. She was more afraid than she had ever been in her life. Her hands shook as she laid out the squirrels.

"Right cozy little place you fixed up here." Barrett broke into her thoughts. "Won't be cozy when winter gets here and the temps drop below zero. Did you plan to tough it out? I don't think the old man has it in him to survive the winter. He's lookin' awful frail."

Sydney looked up from her chore, her mouth hanging open with surprise. Did Barrett think that she wanted to make casual conversation with him? She gave her head a brief shake and returned to her task.

Barrett leaped to his feet and crossed the cave floor in half a second. He slapped her hard, and then slapped her again.

Sydney fell to the cave floor. She lifted her hands to her burning cheeks. Although she feared he would strike her a third time, she forced herself to sit up and look him in the eye.

"Don't ignore me." Barrett's voice was tight with anger. "Your life's in my hands now, and if I want a little talk, you'll give me talk. I ask a question, you answer. Got that?"

He waited for Sydney's nod before returning to the box next to her grandfather. He sat back down and looked at

Sydney. "Let's try again, shall we? Now, were you plannin' to tough out the winter here?"

Sydney shook her head, afraid that her voice wouldn't work. She gulped down the lump in her throat and forced herself to speak, striving to keep her fear out of her voice.

"I-I don't know. My grandfather is too weak to move so I don't think I have much choice."

She focused her attention back on the squirrels. She had always enjoyed preparing wild game and prided herself on doing a neat job of it.

She made short work of cleaning them, placing the unusable parts in a bowl. She then worked her fingers between the flesh and body and separated the skin from the meat. When she was finished skinning them she set them on a short plank of wood to keep them out of the dirt and stood.

"There's dry wood behind you," she said.

Barrett turned and saw a small neat pile of firewood stacked against the cave wall. He stood and moved a few steps out of Sydney's way, but stayed close to her grandfather.

Sydney understood his wordless threat: if she dared to try anything her grandfather would pay. She crossed the floor and chose what she needed from the pile, all the while keeping her eye on the club in Barrett's hand.

She grabbed a fistful of dried grasses and pine twigs that she used for tinder and laid everything in the stove. There were a few coals from the morning's fire and the tinder caught right away. She added larger wood and fanned the flames until she was certain the fire was burning well.

She put a small amount of water in a pan and set it on top of the stove, added the squirrels, and covered it to braise them. It was a meager and boring dish, but the days of having fresh vegetables and spices to liven meals were long past. At least there was meat and it would be hot.

She had a feeling she wouldn't be eating any of it.

Sydney returned to the back corner of the cave and sat on the floor to wait for the squirrels to cook. She tried to force all thoughts from her mind. She knew that if she allowed herself to think about her situation she would succumb to her fear, and her fear would paralyze her.

The cave filled with the sour stench of Barrett's unwashed body. She studied him out of the corner of her eye. He was stronger than she had expected. She remembered the feel of his hard chest and arms. She knew that she wouldn't be able to overpower him physically.

If she was going to have any chance at escape, she would need to surprise him. Her grandfather was still sleeping and that concerned her. With all the noise and activity around him he should have woken by now.

"Time to break out the hooch I think." Barrett was enjoying himself. He and Cal had been traveling rough for a long time, with not enough to eat most days, and only each other for company.

He eyed the girl on the floor. "You don't have many curves but yer pretty enough in the face."

Sydney blushed under Barrett's scrutiny, looked away and bit her lower lip. "I'm sorry. I lied to you. We don't have any alcohol."

Barrett gave her a hard look and then took the knife and pressed the blade to her grandfather's face. Several drops of blood oozed out and slid down his cheek. The old man whimpered in his sleep.

"That's for lyin' to me. Do it again and next time I'll cut off one of his fingers. Understand?"

Sydney nodded. She had no choice but to do as he asked.

Hatred for her disgusting captor filled her heart and replaced her fear.

"Cal wasn't as tough as he thought he was," said Barrett, his tone conversational. "I think maybe you did me a favor when you pushed him over the cliff. Now I don't have to share you, do I? I woulda had to get rid of him anyway, he had a softness in him. Thought he was smarter than me and he didn't enjoy killin' as much as I do. Take off your clothes."

Sydney's head jerked up in shock. Barrett's request took her by surprise. *Take off her clothes? Now? In front of her grandfather?* She started to shake her head no.

Barrett saw the small movement and gave her an evil grin. He stood, and despite her resolve to show no fear, Sydney cowered, afraid that he was going to strike her again.

He nodded with satisfaction. "I see yer startin' to understand. I will hurt you, it don't matter to me when. One way or another, you ain't goin' to live through this day anyhow."

Numb with shock, Sydney stood and slowly unbuttoned her blouse. She shrugged it off. She unsnapped her jeans, then slowly unzipped them.

She had dreamed of doing this one day with someone she loved—the slow, seductive act of undressing for a special man. This felt nothing like her dream.

She hooked her thumbs into her waistband and slid the jeans over her hips, letting them drop to the cave floor. She stepped out of them and stood in her bra and panties.

"Go on, all of it." He pressed the knife against her grandfather's pinky finger.

Sydney swallowed. Her fingers trembled as she unhooked the clasp of her bra and slid it off her shoulders. She shivered when the cool air of the cave hit her bare breasts. Her panties soon joined the pile of clothes at her feet.

She stood naked and stared at the rug. She couldn't look

at Barrett or her grandfather. She was embarrassed and felt incredibly vulnerable without her clothes. Her hands crept up and she crossed her arms over her breasts, tried to cover herself. Goosebumps covered her body and she shivered in spite of the heat that wafted off the stove.

"I've seen me better," Barrett said as he took a step closer to Sydney. "I like them bigger in the booby department but your legs are better than any show girl's. Turn around. I want to see it all."

Sydney had no choice but to comply. She turned her back to Barrett. She expected him to knock her on the back of the head at any moment. She wanted to throw up, to race out of the cave and run away. The desire to flee made her muscles tense.

"Mmm, mmmm. Yessiree, nice booty. What's your name anyway? I like to know who I'm doin' the dirty with, ya know?"

"Sydney." The word came out half-croak, half-whisper. She stared at the cave wall in front of her, unwilling to turn around.

"Sidney? That's a boy's name. What were your folks thinking?"

"It's spelled with a y, that's the female version." Sydney didn't seem able to speak above a whisper.

She heard Barrett move behind her and she braced herself for his touch. She broke out in a cold sweat. He was so close that she could feel his hot breath on her bare shoulders. A wave of shudders shook her body.

"What's the matter, Sydney with a y?" Barrett whispered into her ear. "This yer first time? I promise you it'll be an experience you'll never forget." He cackled, then grabbed her shoulder and spun her around to face him.

Sydney was horrified to see that he had removed his

pants. She jerked her eyes back up to his face. Barrett wore a wide leer and his eye was hard. He looked more like a cyclops monster than a man.

She willed herself not to panic and run. Somehow she had to survive this assault and rescue her grandfather. She swallowed back the bile that choked her throat and shut off her mind.

Barrett put his hands on Sydney's shoulders and forced her down to the floor. He knelt down and roughly pushed her onto her back, then pressed down on one of her shoulders to hold her there.

The rugs she had so carefully placed on the cave floor cushioned her body from the hard dirt. She wished they weren't there. She'd rather feel the cold, hard earth. It was more suitable for what she was about to endure.

Barrett forced her knees apart with his own. The look on his face had grown cruel and ugly.

Sydney closed her eyes to shut his face out. She didn't want the image of this human animal haunting her dreams.

Barrett grabbed her left breast and squeezed hard. He cackled again, his vile breath washing over her.

Sydney cried out from the pain. She opened her eyes and stared at the rough sandstone ceiling of the cave. Such a warm gold color sprinkled with sparkles.

Is this how her sister felt as she looked at the sky those last few minutes? Shannon, I'll be with you soon.

6

SYDNEY CAUGHT a movement in the corner of her eye. She shifted her gaze beyond Barrett and saw her grandfather standing by his chair, a look of fury on his creased, white-whiskered face.

He shuffled a couple of unsteady steps, lifted his walking stick, and whacked Barrett on the back of his head with the ram's head.

Barrett jumped off Sydney with a howl and swiped at her grandfather's legs, knocking him down. Sydney heard her grandfather's head hit the stove before he collapsed on the cave floor and lay still.

Something cold and dark and dangerous awoke in her.

She rolled to her side, grabbed a cast iron fry pan, and swung it at the back of Barrett's head, putting all her weight behind it.

The fry pan connected with a soft thud and Barrett fell to the cave floor. Hatred for Barrett and the men who had raped and murdered Shannon filled Sydney. She brought the fry pan down on his head again. The distinct, coppery smell of blood filled the cave.

Barrett lay unmoving, the back of his head a mass of bloody flesh.

Sydney's breaths stuttered from her in harsh sobs. She stood over Barrett's body, the fry pan held ready to wipe out any remaining sign of life. After several minutes she realized Barrett was dead and she dropped her trembling arms.

She turned away from the dead man and went to her grandfather. She rolled him over gently but she could tell that he too was dead. She held him against her naked body and cried deep, wrenching sobs until her throat was raw and her insides ached with the pain of her loss.

Dusk had fallen by the time Sydney's tears dried up. She knew that the smell of blood in the cave would soon attract the hungry night scavengers.

She forced herself to her feet, put on her clothes, tied Barrett's wrists together over his head to give her something to hold onto, and pulled his body sideways on the rug.

Twice she was forced to stop and run outside to vomit. She steeled herself to handle the dead man. She needed to hold herself together long enough to dispose of the body.

Sydney rolled Barrett inside the rug, leaving his tied hands together and sticking out of one end. She tied a piece of rope around the rug at each end to hold it all together like a giant sausage, and then grabbed his already cold hands and dragged the body from the cave.

She humped Barrett's body, inches at a time, along the trail to the point where she had pushed Cal to his death. It was slow, hard work. By the time she reached the landslide, the sun was below the horizon and the cool night air helped clear her head.

Sydney removed the rope from the rug and pushed Barrett off the trail. There was no point in wasting a good piece of rope—especially as there were no hardware stores left to buy a replacement.

A barred owl called from the valley below her and she could just make out the small brown bats already flitting about catching insects in the waning twilight.

She watched Barrett's body bounce down the steep hillside, the rug unrolling as he fell. Freed from the rug, he hung up on a small poplar tree, and then slid free and fell several hundred feet further before coming to rest in a rock pile. A cold hardness filled her as she looked at the two bodies below.

Good riddance to bad rubbish.

Sydney knew the coyotes who hunted the land around her cave would find the bodies during the night. The crows and vultures would move in tomorrow to pick at the carcasses, and then the insects would do a final cleanup. In a few days Barrett and Cal would be nothing more than bones and a bad memory.

Barrett had killed her grandfather and deserved to die. He especially deserved to have his body torn apart by wild animals. Her only regret was that he wouldn't be alive to experience it.

She stared at the bodies and thought about how Cal and Barrett had changed her life. They had taken from her everything she cared about. They had turned her into a killer, no better than the men she had killed.

When it became too dark to see the bodies any longer she reluctantly headed back to the cave and her grandfather. Along the way Sydney puzzled over what to do about her grandfather's body.

She did not want him to be devoured by the wild scavengers, yet there was no place to bury him on the bluff. The ground had only a thin covering of topsoil. She didn't think she was strong enough to carry him back to the farm to bury alongside Shannon.

Unable to sleep because she feared dreams of Cal and Barrett, Sydney sat with her grandfather's body through the long night. In the morning she forced herself to choke down the braised squirrels. She needed to eat if she hoped to survive.

Every now and then a dry sob would rack her body. She wrapped her arms around her chest, as if by physically holding on, she could hold her emotions together.

She was truly alone now, and she didn't know what to do. Caring for her grandfather had given Sydney something to focus on after Shannon's murder, and now he was gone.

She felt lost, adrift without anything to grab on to. If only her parent's had returned, none of this would have happened. Her sister and grandfather would still be alive, and Sydney would not be alone.

Alone, alone, alone. The word kept repeating in her brain: an unwanted mantra of despair. She, Sydney Waters, the girl who always had dreams, had lost her ability to think, to come up with a plan of action.

She spent two days in the cave sitting beside her grandfather's body. Barrett's dried blood flaked and itched on her skin but she didn't notice. Slowly the will to survive ebbed away and the desire to join her family took its place.

She wrapped herself in a blanket and lay beside her grandfather and waited. The cave was as good a place to die as any.

"*Sydney.*"

Sydney heard her name and struggled to open her eyes. Who had called her name?

"*Sydney. This is not your time. Your grandfather was old and crippled, he was ready to pass on. You must not waste this life, there is still much for you to experience.*"

She managed to open her eyes but she had trouble getting them to focus. She thought she saw someone standing in the cave, but the image wavered and made her feel ill. She closed her eyes again.

"*SYDNEY. Get up! This is not your time to die.*"

"I have nothing to live for." Her throat was dry and sore and the words came out in a hoarse whisper.

She tried to open her eyes again. Smokey stood before her. She wormed one hand out of her blanket and reached for him but he moved off. She could see the cave wall through his translucent body.

When she focused on his face, Smokey disappeared. Sydney pulled her hand inside the blanket and fell back to sleep.

On the third day she awoke from a vivid dream. In the dream, Smokey was teaching her as he had taught her the summer that seemed a lifetime ago now, teaching her about his shaman grandmother's view of the world and life.

As she lay there thinking about the dream, it occurred to her that she could go to Smokey. She would tell Smokey about failing Shannon and her grandfather. About killing two men in cold blood.

Perhaps after her confession she could die in peace.

Sydney rolled up onto her knees and tried to stand. Weak from lack of food and water, it took several attempts to get to her feet as her legs kept buckling underneath her. She needed to eat but there was nothing in the cave.

Sydney crawled to her grandfather's chair and pulled herself up with its support. She took several sips of water and kept it down, fighting the cramps in her stomach and the urge to vomit.

She knew the dangers of dehydration. She had drank very little since deciding to die and needed to replenish her body's fluids. She forced herself to take slow, small sips until her stomach felt full.

A mature hickory tree grew not far from the cave. If the squirrels and turkeys hadn't already cleaned up all the nuts she could gather enough to take the edge off her hunger.

She had to stop every few minutes to rest as she made her way down the bluff to the tree. Her progress was agonizingly slow and she was afraid that she had waited too long; what if she didn't have the energy to gather enough food to keep herself alive?

She misstepped and tumbled down the hillside, her fall stopped short by an oak tree. She lay against the oak and whimpered while she gathered the energy to continue.

When she reached the hickory tree she dropped to her hands and knees to search through the dead leaves for the small, white nuts. It was easier to crawl on all fours than to walk.

When Sydney found a nut she placed it on a flat rock and smashed it with a smaller one. The nut disintegrated into a mishmash of shell and meat. It was frustrating work to separate the two but she patiently picked out pieces of nutmeat and ate them.

She stayed at the hickory tree for the remainder of the day, gathering and eating tiny bits of the sweet nut, and napping next to the tree's trunk when she became too exhausted. The sweet smell of the leaves and earth began to replace the smell of blood that lay trapped in her sinuses.

The sun dipped low in the sky, and Sydney decided to spend the night with the tree rather than expend the energy to climb back to the cave. She gathered armloads of leaves and piled them next to a large, downed elm tree. She broke some cedar boughs, apologizing to the trees as she did so, and placed several over the leaves. She leaned the remainder against the downed tree to form a makeshift shelter. She piled more leaves on top of the boughs and crawled inside. It was snug and protected and she fell asleep instantly.

The next morning Sydney filled her pockets with nuts and slowly made her way back to the cave. She smelled her grandfather's body before she reached the cave's entrance. It was time to bury her dead and move on.

Sydney spent the remainder of the morning making plans and drawing up lists of things that she might need for her journey to find Smokey. She searched through the cave and collected a small pile of items to take with her: her down sleeping bag, a few pieces of clothing, her crossbow, a knife, her favorite water bottle and a small fry pan to cook in.

She would gather the rest of the items that she needed from the farm.

She moved her meager belongings to a spot outside the cave and began to gather stones to seal up the cave entrance. The task seemed to take forever. When she first found the cave she had gathered all the nearby stones to build the wall. Now she was forced to search farther afield which took more time and used up her precious energy.

Slow and steady, she kept at it until she had collected a sufficient pile of stones. She returned to her grandfather and gently covered his body with his favorite blanket. She took down the canvas door flap and began to stack rocks in the cave's entrance first. When the enclosure was thigh-high she stopped.

This was the last time she would ever see any of her family. She scrambled over the partial wall back into the cave, and stood beside her grandfather's body. Her intellect told her she had to leave him, this body was but a shell, and a deteriorating one at that, but her heart was unwilling to let go.

"You deserve better, Pops, but this is the best I can do." She bent down and picked up her grandfather's walking stick. "I'm going to take this to remember you by. Not that I would ever forget."

She climbed back out of the cave, anxious now to be on her way. She finished walling up the entryway and then closed in the air space at the top of the wall, sealing her grandfather's body inside his sandstone tomb.

Satisfied that she had protected her grandfather from scavengers, Sydney leaned her forehead against the walled up entrance.

"Bye, Pops. Thanks for saving me from that monster. I love you. At least I know you're with Mom and Dad and Shannon and you're all at peace. Wish me luck."

Sydney stood on the trail for several more minutes, suddenly unable to leave. The cave was not much of a home, but it was familiar and all she had left.

Finally, with a deep sigh and a heavy heart, she put on the pack with her meager supplies and started down the bluff trail.

She planned to take no more than one day to finish gathering what she needed from the farm, and then she'd be on her way. She hoped that everything was waiting where she had left it.

7

SYDNEY SMELLED the farmhouse before she saw it. The aroma of damp, scorched wood reached her in the woods that separated the old farm fields from the bluff. She circled the area around the house twice to make sure she was alone before she dared to step out of the tree cover.

She went first to her sister's grave. A buttercup squash seed had sprouted and covered the mound with its large leaves, golden yellow blossoms, and mix of ripe and green fruit. Sydney gave a wry smile at the sight. Mom would like knowing that Shannon was now a part of her garden.

The squash plant prompted her to search the old garden plot for other volunteer vegetables that she could scavenge. She found a few tomatoes, a couple of onions, potatoes, and several perennial herbs: enough for a vegetable stew.

She built a small fire from wood that she pulled off the remains of the house and set an oven grate across two logs. The wind-driven well pump still worked and she filled two pots: one for her stew and one for a sponge bath.

When the water was hot enough, Sydney stripped off her clothes and gave herself a thorough scrubbing with a towel rag. Relieved to finally rid herself of Barrett's dried blood, her spirits began to lift.

She emptied the pot of now-pink water and heated another. By the time she finished the second wash she felt cleansed of some of the horror of her encounter with Cal and Barrett.

Her skin grew rosy from the vigorous scrubbing. She heated a third pot of water and washed all her clothes, then spread them in the sun to dry. Still weak from lack of food and exhausted from the emotional drain of the previous few days, she spread her sleeping bag in the sun to air, and then lay down on top of it.

The sun's rays warmed her newly cleaned skin. She fell into a deep and dreamless sleep and woke several hours later feeling refreshed and hungry.

While she waited for her vegetable stew to cook, Sydney checked on the trunk that she had left hidden behind the old hay barn. She was relieved to find it sitting where she'd left it, under a leaning tree trunk with brush piled over it, the padlock still in place.

The hot stew and familiar surroundings of home restored her energy and her spirits. Clean, and with a full belly, she slept more soundly than she had since Shannon's death.

As Sydney ate more of the reheated stew for breakfast she considered her travel plans. She had never been to Smokey's and had only a general idea of where he lived.

She found an atlas in the house and studied the states she would have to pass through to get to the town near where Smokey lived. The best route would take her through the dry plains states and then along the eastern edge of the Rockies.

Drinking water would be her biggest problem. She could survive without food for a few days, but she needed water daily and she wouldn't be able to carry much. That meant that she had to plan her route close to streams and rivers.

She remembered reading *Undaunted Courage* in her teens, the story of Lewis and Clark's courageous journey through the uncharted western United States. The journey she planned to make would be equally difficult, maybe even more so as she was a lone female traveler and the explorers had traveled with a band of armed men.

She checked the scale on the maps and her heart sank. The distances she faced were daunting. It would be more than fifteen hundred miles on foot; a long, dangerous journey with no guarantee that she would find Smokey at the end.

Sydney looked around her. Robins and song sparrows were singing, the sun was shining, and she sat warm and comfortable with a full belly. The farm's gardens could be easily resurrected if she could find seeds. The tools she needed were still in the garden shed. She could hunt game and cure the meat in the smokehouse. She could fortify one of the structurally sound rooms in the house and make it livable, or create a secure spot in one of the barns.

The farm sat off the main road, tucked in a deep valley, and the road that led to the farm was now overgrown with weeds and grass. The chance of her being discovered again were slim.

Perhaps she should stay here for the winter at least. It would be the safest and easiest thing to do. Maybe she was foolish to want to leave at all.

Sydney thought of Shannon and her grandfather's body lying in the cave. The burden of their deaths weighed heavily on her heart. *There's no future for me here, only death. It's time to leave.* Her resolve strengthened, she returned her attention to the maps to plan her route.

Sydney decided to stay at the farm for a few extra days to make her preparations. She had enough volunteer vegetables from the garden to make several stews and she knew it was important to build up her strength before she began the long trek. The delay in setting out would give her time to hunt and smoke some meat, as well as catch up on her sleep.

She would be limited by how much weight she could carry on her back. She needed food, water, a pot to cook in, a dish and a cup, her sleeping bag, hunting tools, extra clothing, a tarp for a ground cloth, something to protect her from the weather, the necessary maps, maybe other things she hadn't thought of yet.

She set out the next morning to look for game. Smoking meat took time so it was first on her list of preparations. Her thoughts were focused on squirrels when she unexpectedly came across a flock of wild turkeys.

The turkeys would be a welcome change from the squirrel meat she had been eating for the last few months. Unfortunately, with their massive breasts, they were tough to take down with a body shot.

Sydney tried and failed to hit one in the head with her slingshot and she had to admit defeat. She returned to the farm empty-handed and while she rested puzzled over a way to capture one or two of the birds.

Later that day she found her father's cast net stuffed in a small canvas bag. A fishing net constructed from a wide circle of knotted line with weights spaced at intervals around the outer edges, it had a tail that was woven loosely around the entire edge. Many native tribes around the world used a similar design to harvest fish from ponds and lakes.

Sydney's father had demonstrated the net's use for her

one day at their farm pond. He had gathered up the net with both hands and then flung it wide across the water, where it spread across the surface like a giant, transparent jellyfish. Her father held onto the tail and waited for it to sink, then jerked it hard, gathering the net into a sacklike form and trapping the fish inside.

Sydney eyed the net now and thought about the turkeys. Perhaps there was a way to capture one with the net. She took a small box and set it on the ground for a target. At first she couldn't get the net to spread wide. Every time she tossed it refused to spread out into a circle; it hung together in a useless clump instead.

She tried gathering it differently and moved her hands farther apart. The net spread into a half circle. Encouraged, Sydney kept practicing until she could consistently make the net spread over the box.

The next morning she was up before the sun and made for the spot where she had seen the turkeys. She knew that the big birds had specific routines. They liked to roost in mature trees at night—but not too high off the ground. They liked to scratch for insects and nuts during the day, and unless threatened they traveled slowly through the forest looking for food.

She searched the trees in the pale gray light until she spotted the flock in their roost. She tested the wind, then slow-walked until she was near the spot she expected them to land when they flew down from the trees. Her slow and silent movements raised no alarm and she got herself set with the net.

The light grew brighter and the turkeys began to move. They ruffled their feathers, stretched their wings, and made soft puck-puck noises. The first two birds off the roost soared well beyond Sydney's spot. Two more joined them. She had miscalculated the distance they would cover.

She decided to stay where she was and was soon rewarded for her decision. A single hen turkey soared off the roost, landed a short distance from Sydney, and began to walk toward her.

Elated, Sydney tensed and readied herself to fling the net. She waited for her prey to reach a spot that was mostly clear of objects that could snag and hang up the net, and then tossed it.

The net landed on the hen turkey and Sydney jerked the line to enclose the bird, but the net wouldn't pull tight. The turkey beat its large wings and squawked, struggling to free itself. It began to run, dragging the net with it. Sydney scrambled after the bird and flung herself on top of it. The large, strong wings beat in her face as she tried to wrap her arms around them.

The turkey was surprisingly strong. Sydney lost her hold on it and had to scramble when the bird freed itself from her grasp. The bird began to run. Desperate not to lose the meat she needed for her trip, Sydney pulled her knife and threw herself on top of the hen again. This time she quickly sliced its throat. Within moments the bird lay unmoving underneath her.

A sharp stab of remorse ran through Sydney. The hen turkey had put up a brave and desperate fight for her life, and she was incredibly beautiful—her feathers reflected iridescent bronze and green in the early morning sunlight.

"This animal sacrificed its life so that you may live." Smokey's words came to her, told her what to do. *"Always thank the animal's spirit for its gift of life."*

"Thank you beautiful Mother Turkey for your sacrifice. I

will not waste your precious gift." Sydney gathered up the net, put it into her pack, and carried her prize home.

Back at the farm, Sydney gathered green hickory wood for the smokehouse and arranged it in the smokehouse fire pit. She carefully cleaned the turkey and cut the meat into thin strips, then laid them across the smokehouse racks, started the fire, and closed the door.

She placed the turkey carcass into her soup pot and put the pot onto her cooking fire. The meat broth would be a welcome change and help build up her strength. While her soup cooked she gathered more things that she might need for the journey.

Sydney and Shannon had camped with their parents from the time they were four years old. She felt confident she knew what she needed to survive the upcoming journey. Her biggest concern was making sure she had the appropriate clothing, shoes, and stockings. With the miles she needed to cover, blisters could be a big issue. Maintaining healthy feet was a necessity.

After several hours of rummaging she came up with an assortment of clothing. She discarded her mother's bulky winter jacket and decided to rely on layers for warmth. She also discarded any polar fleece pieces and settled on a wool shirt and a wool sweater instead.

Unlike the fleece, the wool would keep her warm even when it got wet, and paired with a down vest and waterproof windbreaker it would be enough to keep her warm in the snow.

She found two pair of her mother's favorite camo army pants, a pair of rain pants, and two pair of long underwear: one in silk and one in wool.

Footwear was a bigger issue. She stopped and ate a bowl

of turkey broth with vegetables while she considered the problem.

She checked on the smokehouse—it was filled with the thick, sweet smell of hickory smoke. Satisfied with her progress so far, Sydney laid out her sleeping bag in the sun and fell into a deep and restful sleep.

A mob of blue jays woke her several hours later with their raucous cries. She stretched lazily but did not get up. The jays were not sounding the alarm and it felt good to relax. The combination of nourishing food, bathing, and sleep had done wonders for her psyche; Sydney felt more at peace than she had since the day of Shannon's death.

She still puzzled over the issue of footwear. She currently wore a pair of outgrown sneakers with the toes cut out to give her feet room. They sufficed for the small amount of walking she had been doing here, but they were woefully inadequate for the long journey ahead.

She dug her old hiking boots out of her bedroom closet but couldn't even squeeze her foot into them. Not surprising, as two years had passed since she last used them.

She searched the hall closet but found only a pair of her grandfather's rubber galoshes; all of her father's shoes and boots had been stolen. She made her way to the rear of the house, where her parent's bedroom had been partially destroyed by the fire. Sydney picked her way carefully through the debris to what remained of their closet and poked through her mother's shoes in vain. There was nothing she could use.

She sighed with frustration. She had no choice but to fortify her sneakers somehow. Perhaps she could fashion something with leather scraps and duct tape, provided she could find either item.

She rummaged through the rest of the house and found a

leather bag that once served as her grandfather's library book bag. She could cut scraps from it and attach them to her sneakers, try to cover her toes.

A search of the house turned up nothing that could be used to attach the leather to her sneakers.

Sydney stood at the head of the cellar stairs. This was the last place to search for items she could use. She tried the cellar door but it had swollen in the frame and would not open. She found a screwdriver and took the screws out of the hinges, then pried the door off and set it aside.

She peered down the stairs; very little light permeated the underground space and it smelled damp and musty. She kept close to the old stone foundation as she took the stairs one at a time, testing each one before she put her full weight on it. When she reached the bottom she stood and gave her eyes time to adjust to the low light.

She spied her father's workbench off to her right and headed for it. If there was any duct tape to be found in the house it would be there. It was darker in this corner of the cellar, and she was forced to search the workbench more by feel than by sight.

She found nothing useful on top of the bench. She squatted down to search the shelf underneath.

Sydney pulled out several boxes of model airplane parts and set them aside. Her father had loved to build and fly remote controlled planes in their hay field. Her hands lingered on a long, smooth wing; she could feel the raised surface of the personal sticker he had created to identify all his planes.

She traced the interwoven letters: A. W. A. — Alex Waters Airlines. Her hands trembled as she set the box aside and reached deeper into the shelf. She touched what felt like curly ribbon and she grasped onto it and pulled it out.

For a moment she didn't comprehend what she held. Then it hit her. This was a present, a gift from her father for her mother's birthday. The family had planned to celebrate it when her mother returned from her trip to New York. Because her mother had a bad habit of searching for her birthday and Christmas gifts, her father had hidden her present in the cellar until her return.

Her quest for duct tape forgotten, Sydney carried the present upstairs and out of the house.

Sydney missed her father terribly. He had never treated her like a child. He talked to her about the wildlife he studied, took her with him to collect water samples, and was always happy to answer her questions without ever making her feel stupid.

She wished that she could crawl into her father's lap now and feel his strong arms around her, feel his flannel shirt against her cheek as she snuggled against his warm body, his deep voice rumbling in his chest against her ear.

Alex Waters had loved both of his daughters, but Sydney loved nature the way he did and spent more time with him. Shannon took after their mother, always working on some artsy project.

"Ah well, Sydney, those days are long gone." Her voice sounded strange to her ears, small and raspy from lack of use. She forced her thoughts back to the present and inspected the still-bright wrapping paper. There was a deep blue envelope taped to the package. Her mother's favorite color. She ran a finger under the flap, opened it and pulled out the card.

"Happy Birthday to my beloved wife and dearest friend. All my love, Alex."

An intense pain gripped Sydney's chest and held tight. For a moment she couldn't draw a breath. She dashed away the tears running down her face and carefully set down the card. Taking immense care to preserve the paper, she unwrapped the gift.

Her heart stuttered when she read the lettering on the box cover. She opened it, hands shaking, and pulled the tissue paper aside. A pair of expensive leather hiking boots lay nestled in the box. Exactly what her mother had requested for her forty-third birthday.

"Oh lord, let them fit, please let them fit."

Sydney took out the left boot and laced it up, removed her sneaker, and pushed her foot into the boot. It was a half size too large, but with socks it would be a perfect fit. She hugged the right boot to her body and squeezed her eyes shut.

"Thank you, Daddy, thank you, Mom, wherever you are. You may have just saved my life."

She laced up the right boot and put it on. The boots were constructed of a beautiful dark brown leather, already water-proofed and waiting to be put to work.

The unexpected find boosted Sydney's confidence. Until the discovery of the boots, she had been preparing for a journey that in her heart she felt was doomed. Now she experienced a glimmer of hope that she might succeed, that she might be able to walk over one thousand miles and find her friend Smokey Greenfeather.

Sydney returned to her preparations with renewed energy, humming under her breath.

Two more days passed.

Finally Sydney felt ready. She had winnowed down the pile of equipment to the bare essentials, much of it taken from her father's camping supplies: an aluminum cook set that separated into a pot, fry pan, and dish, a small water purifier, eating and cooking utensils, a sharpening stone and steel knife, steel and flint to start fires, a small pair of binoculars, a can of waterproofing for the boots.

She added a coil of climbing rope and a set of bungee cords and filled the rest of her backpack with clothing, her sleeping bag, a couple of towels, the smoked, dried turkey strips, and the small tarp. She packed every pair of stockings she could find.

The success of her undertaking would depend upon the health of her feet and keeping them dry would be important. Lastly, she placed her maps, knives, slingshot, and crossbow pistol into the outside pockets.

There was one final task to do before she left. She had debated with herself long and hard, but eventually realized she could never truly leave the farm until she made a large, symbolic change.

The time had come. Her knife was sharp. She stood before the passenger window of her grandfather's old farm truck and took a firm hold of her braid. Grasping it tightly to the side with her left hand, she sawed at it with the knife.

The braid came away in her hand, lifeless now, nothing more than a hair rope. She gulped back a sob and laid the braid on the hood of the truck.

Her thick, black hair had never been cut, and the sudden freedom from the weight of her braid made her head feel light, as if it could float off her neck.

She pulled the half-rusted scissors she had found from her pocket and continued cutting. She felt out of control and slightly frantic, as if by cutting off enough hair she could wipe away all that had happened and become a new person.

She snipped and cut until only a few inches of black curls surrounded her head. Finally she set the scissors down and examined her reflection in the window.

Never again would a man be able to capture her and hold her prisoner by her hair.

Satisfied with the results, she returned to the house and plucked her father's worn, felt crusher hat from the front closet and placed it on her head.

She filled two water bottles from the well and added them to the outside pockets on her pack, then lifted the loaded pack onto her back and adjusted the straps. It was a little heavier than she liked, but she knew that she would get used to carrying the weight.

Sydney spun in a slow circle, took a last look around at her family home, and wondered if she would ever see the place again. She felt a deep sadness for all that had been lost here mixed with excitement for the adventure that lay ahead.

She heaved a deep sigh and headed down the farm road to pick up the trail west.

THE JOURNEY BEGINS

It is good to have an end to journey toward, but it is the journey that matters in the end. Ursula K. Le Guin

8

SYDNEY KNEW that the travelers who stopped by her grandfather's farm mostly followed the main roads and highways. She decided to follow the secondary gravel roads in hopes that she could avoid any confrontations.

Many of the roads between the Mississippi River and the Rockies were laid out in a north-south, east-west grid, a road practically every mile, so it was easy for her to pick up a road that headed straight west.

She planned to cover roughly twenty to twenty-five miles a day, the lower mileage on bad weather days. At that rate and with rest days, she figured it would take her almost two months to reach Smokey's home in Wyoming.

She concentrated on putting one foot in front of another and quickly settled into a comfortable walking rhythm. It felt good to be moving, to have a sense of purpose. She no longer minded being alone. The solitude felt peaceful and restful after the trauma she had left behind.

The dried turkey would sustain her for at least two weeks if she rationed it, and this part of Iowa had numerous small streams she could use to refill her water bottles. As she got further west access to water would become an issue. She began to fret about water but stopped herself; she would deal with the problems as they arose. "No sense inviting trouble," her grandfather used to say.

The weather was dry and clear and Sydney soon established a daily routine. She got up with the sun, ate a little turkey as she walked, took a break midday and ate again, rested a short while and changed into dry socks, then walked until near dark when she looked for a safe place to spend the night.

Finding places to sleep that felt safe was a challenge. The first three nights she slept in the tree rows on the edges of abandoned farm fields. She avoided the farm buildings because she figured other travelers would be drawn to them for shelter and she didn't want to be trapped inside one with strangers.

The fields, once covered with vast acres of corn and soybeans, alfalfa and oats, now held opportunistic weeds like thistle, goldenrod, and cow parsnip.

She was careful not to touch the cow parsnip. As a young girl she had learned the hard way that the plant's sap produced a painful skin rash.

Errant cornstalks popped up through the weeds, and although they were a flavorless, bred-for-livestock-variety, Sydney picked an occasional ear and cooked it to augment her smoked turkey.

There were times when only the flat abandoned farm fields separated the interstate highway from the gravel roads that Sydney walked. Sunlight reflected off the windshields of vehicles left parked on Interstate 90's breakdown lane, and she even saw cars abandoned in the middle of the road when they had run out of gas.

Twice she spotted a knot of travelers moving slowly

along the interstate. The first time she hid in a ditch until the travelers were out of sight and there was no chance of them spotting her.

She came upon the second group of travelers as they were sitting by the roadside. She didn't notice them until she was almost abreast with the group. Even with the field separating them it was far too close for safety's sake.

She bent over to make herself less noticeable against the horizon and sought the cover and protection of a tree row.

She changed directions and followed the trees south, planning to pick up the next westbound gravel road a mile south of the one she was on, but found herself in the back yard of a large farmhouse before she reached the road she sought. She paused at the edge of the yard and waited, looking and listening for signs of occupants.

The farm had three barns and several assorted outbuildings, all standing intact. This farm, once prosperous, had escaped the tornadoes and violent hail storms that had destroyed so many others. Weeds now filled the surrounding fields and yard.

Sydney moved slowly to her left, keeping inside the stand of trees. She stopped in the shadow of a large cottonwood tree and took off her pack with as little movement as possible. She leaned it against the tree, then sat with her back against the rough-barked trunk.

She decided to wait for the cover of night to move again. She made herself comfortable and went to sleep.

"Damn you, Torrie, why'd you have to up and die on me?"

The voice, followed by the sound of a shovel hitting a rock, woke Sydney. She remained frozen in place until she realized the speaker wasn't talking to her. Cautiously she got to her feet and peered around the massive tree trunk.

A man was digging behind the farmhouse, not fifty yards

away from the cottonwood where Sydney stood. Beside him sat the largest dog she had ever seen in her life. The dog had long black and brown fur with patches of white on its face. Even sitting, its massive head reached above the man's waist.

Sydney let out a quiet breath, thankful that she was upwind of the pair. She didn't fancy being torn apart by an animal, and she felt certain the dog would treat her as the intruder she was and attack her.

The man's digging was slow and laborious, as though he had never wielded a shovel before. There were sweat stains on his shirt, not surprising in the late afternoon heat.

Sydney remained motionless. Cicadas buzzed high in the tree over her head. A fat bumblebee wallowed around her legs, bumped into her, and went on its way. A red squirrel stopped in the branches overhead and scolded her, then it too went on its way.

The dog sat frozen, a magnificent canine statue. Besides the man, the insects and the squirrel were the only things in motion. Finally the man stopped digging and threw down the shovel. He leaned down and groped for a long bundle wrapped in a sheet.

Sydney hadn't noticed the bundle—her attention had been wholly riveted on the dog. She realized that the man was burying someone. A wave of sadness passed through her. She wondered who had died and hoped it was a painless death.

The man rolled the body into the hole. The dog whined. The man pressed the dog's head into his side and stroked an ear. "We did all we could, Dogma, but it wasn't enough, she's gone." He felt around for the shovel with one foot, located it, and began to fill in the hole.

Hours passed and evening was fast approaching. Sydney remained standing. She had never before stood without moving some body part for such a long stretch of time. Her legs were stiff and tired and her arms felt like weights at her side, but she was afraid to even twitch.

She needed to wait until full dark, when she expected the man and dog to go inside the house, before she dared to navigate her way through their yard.

The man finished covering the body and then dropped to his knees. He began to sing, the words at first garbled and soft. They grew clearer and stronger and reached Sydney's ears. He had a deep, smooth voice.

> *"You were my sunlight,*
> *My moon and star light,*
> *You pierced the darkness,*
> *Made things all right,*
> *Your love and friendship,*
> *Were all I needed,*
> *Thank you my sister,*
> *The light of my life."*

The man's head dropped and his heavy sobs filled the yard. The dog stayed at his side and howled in accompaniment.

Their pain cut through Sydney and made her shiver. She felt embarrassed to bear witness to such deep grief; she was violating the stranger's right to express his pain in private. She hung her head so she wouldn't have to watch—she could at least give him that.

After a while the sobs died and the yard grew quiet again. The sun was a glowing red ball on the horizon, the clouds painted purple-gray. Stars were beginning to twinkle overhead and a great-horned owl hooted softly in the distance. The sunset brought a breeze and cooler air, raising goose-bumps on Sydney's arms.

"I know you're there, you know."

Startled, Sydney's head snapped up. Was the man talking to her?

"Over by the big tree, I know you're there." The man grabbed the dog's ruff and pulled himself to his feet.

Sydney grabbed her pack and stepped behind the tree.

"You might as well come here, Dogma can outrun any human. If you don't come, I'll tell her to fetch you."

Sydney hesitated, but she knew the man was right—she couldn't outrun the dog. She shouldered her pack and stepped out from behind the tree, keenly aware that the dog's eyes, reflecting what little light remained, watched her closely.

The man kept his hand entwined in its thick fur and waited.

She walked slowly towards the pair and stopped ten feet away. The fresh grave stood between them. She smelled the freshly turned earth, the scent of death. It brought back the memory of burying her sister, something she didn't want to think about.

"Who was it?" she asked, nodding toward the grave. Her voice was husky and cracked from disuse. It was difficult to make out the man's features in the waning light. She had the impression that he was in his mid-to-late twenties, not much older than Sydney herself.

"My older sister. Who are you?"

"Sydney Waters. I was just passing through. I was trying to avoid a group of travelers and I ended up in your yard without realizing it. I don't want to trouble you in your time of loss."

She didn't dare to walk off, afraid that the man would set the dog on her. She waited. The hours of standing were catching up with her legs; they started to tremble with fatigue. She took a deep breath and willed them to be still.

For several long minutes the man said nothing. He seemed to be thinking something over, but she couldn't tell for sure. The thought was only a sensation as it was now too dark for her to see his face. No light came from any of the buildings. Stars now peppered the sky.

She took another deep breath and let it out, wished the man would say something.

"My name is Jordan James. That's my sister Torrie in the grave. Would you like to join me for dinner? I could use a diversion tonight."

Surprised and flustered by the invitation, Sydney hesitated to accept. The man and dog seemed harmless enough, but she felt reluctant to trust them.

Her stomach growled and reminded her that she was hungry. What a treat it would be to eat something besides dried turkey. "Sure, I guess. Why not? Thank you."

"Follow us." Jordan and Dogma turned and walked together toward one of the outbuildings. Jordan kept his fingers tangled in Dogma's ruff.

Sydney hesitated a moment. Why weren't they headed toward the house? Then she remembered the travelers and realized that living in a house out here on the open plain would be an invitation for trouble. *He must live in one of the smaller outbuildings.*

She fell into step behind the pair, wrinkling her nose at the man's body odor. He smelled like the inside of a chicken coop.

They passed two small, identical sheds set side by side.

Sydney heard the quiet chatter of hens in one and her stomach growled louder. Chicken soup! Hard-boiled eggs!

Her mind conjured up images of bowls filled with hot, steaming food. She almost groaned aloud with the anticipation of a hot meal.

Jordan and Dogma stopped beside a metal Quonset-style building with a low, curved roof. "Don't let the size deceive you," he said as he opened the door and waited for Sydney to grope her way inside. "It's our tornado shelter. Torrie fixed it up real nice. It's really quite comfortable. Mind your step, the stairs start just inside the entrance."

Sydney cautiously slid a foot forward and felt for the first step. It was cave-dark inside the building. She did not want to fall down a set of stairs and suffer a sprained ankle or broken leg. "How do you see in here?" she asked. She took the step slowly.

"Don't worry. There are candles in the shelter. There used to be a light just inside the door but with no electricity it's useless. Just take the steps slow and you'll be fine. Once you start down the stairs you can use the wall to your left to help guide you."

Sydney felt for the wall. It helped steady her balance and she relaxed slightly. She reached the bottom and waited for Jordan and Dogma to join her. They weren't on the stairs. She heard and felt a trapdoor slam shut over her head.

"Hey! What are you doing?"

9

THE UNDERGROUND SPACE muffled her shout. Sydney dropped her pack and groped her way back up the steps until she bumped her head. She felt the rough underside of the floor boards with her hands and searched for a handle. She crouched and pushed against the trapdoor with her shoulders. It didn't budge even a tiny bit.

Sydney pounded on the trapdoor with her fist. Dirt and debris fell onto her face and made her cough.

"Jordan! Let me out! You can't hold me prisoner, it's against the law."

She heard a chuckle on the other side of the door.

"What law? Besides, who's going to find out?"

Sydney sat on the steps and tried to kick at the trapdoor with her feet, averting her face to avoid the dirt. Panic welled up in her. What if that hadn't been a sister that Jordan just buried? What if it was another helpless woman he had trapped and then murdered? Her panic increased and Sydney began to kick harder.

"Be quiet a moment and I'll explain."

Sydney stopped kicking at the door. She knew that it was

futile and she didn't want to ruin the toes of her mother's boots.

"That's better. I need your help, you see. Because I can't. See, that is. I'm blind. My sister took care of me after my parents died, but she got hurt a couple weeks ago. She slipped and fell on a rusty piece of machinery and the wound got infected and she had a fever and I couldn't do anything to help her because I couldn't see. Torrie died because I couldn't see to help her."

Jordan's words were rushed and sounded a little garbled through the thick door, but Sydney understood them well enough. Anger replaced her panic.

She was being held prisoner by a blind nut case who thought he could keep her to replace his now-deceased personal slave.

"I won't survive without help," Jordan continued. "Where were you going, anyway? It's dangerous out there, anywhere you go. You might as well stay here with me and we'll both survive. We have meat and eggs and a small garden. Torrie canned food so we could eat through the winter. You can do that too. You'll come to understand that it makes sense to stay here with me. Just think it over. I'll let you out in a few days."

"A few days!" Sydney's panic returned. "I'll die down here. You're a crackbrain, Jordan James. A certifiable loony. I want to get out now."

"You won't die down there. Torrie kept the shelter well-stocked. In this part of the world you have to be prepared for tornadoes, they don't give much warning. There's food and water and I'm sure she has candles down there for her own use. I never needed them but she didn't like being stuck in the dark."

Sydney didn't blame the dead sister for wanting a light

source in this dark hole. She decided to try a different tack. "I have to pee. Can I please come out? We'll talk about your problem, I promise."

"There's a five-gallon bucket with a lid down there. Use that, that's what it's for. C'mon Dogma, let's go get some sleep, it's been a long shitty day."

"Jordan? Jordan! You bastard! LET. ME. OUT. Where do you think you're going? For heaven's sake, don't leave me here. Jordan!"

"Tsk, tsk, Mr. Waters. Such colorful language for a young man. I can assure you I am no bastard. My parents were well married by the time they had me. I'll let you out when you're ready to meet my terms."

"I'm not a boy!" She heard only silence from the other side of the door. Jordan had left her alone. "Well, this is a fine pickle you've gotten yourself into, Syd. What are you going to do now?" Sydney's words were swallowed up by the underground storm shelter.

She remained sitting near the top of the stairs until she realized that she really did have to pee. She scooted down the stairs using her hands and bottom to feel her way until she felt the hard-packed dirt floor beneath her feet.

There was no light at all in the shelter; she couldn't even see her hand when she held it only inches from her face. She stood and stretched her arms out in front of her and to the sides and felt nothing but air.

She took two steps to the left and repeated the process until she felt rough vertical boards: a wall.

She turned to her right and felt her way along the wall until she came to shelving. Slowly, inch by inch, she felt along each shelf until her fingers came upon a smooth tapered cylinder. She picked it up and held it near her nose;

it had a waxy smell and a short string at one end. She had found a candle.

She groped on the shelf near the candle and found a box of wooden matches. The first match snapped in two when she tried to strike it, but the second one flared. She tilted it to catch the flame and held it to the candlewick. It caught, flickered, then steadied. Sydney held it up and looked around her prison.

Jordan made his way to the back of the farmhouse, his hand tightly wound in Dogma's ruff. He felt repulsed by what he had just done, but he had panicked. He climbed the back steps and reached for the doorknob with his free hand.

Once inside, Jordan found his way to his cot and sat. He dropped his head into his hands and choked out a half-sob. What had he done? Kidnapping a young teen was the act of a desperate man. Judging by Sid's height and voice, he figured the boy was in his early teens—thirteen, or maybe fourteen at the most.

"Torrie, why did you have to die?" The hole his sister's death had left in his life felt enormous. The hole her absence left inside of him seemed like a bottomless chasm.

Torrie had been not only his helpmate, but his best and closest friend. She traveled with him, managed his concerts and recoding sessions, made sure he ate and dressed appropriately. In essence she made it possible for him to survive.

"Dogma, what are we going to do?" He reached for the dog that was never far from his side and buried his tears in her thick fur. When his grief abated he sat and stared into the darkness that never left him. With Torrie at his side the blindness had been bearable. Without her it felt like an insurmountable handicap.

He couldn't leave the farm if he couldn't see where he was going. One misstep into a deep ditch and he could drown, or die from a broken leg.

He couldn't live alone on the farm either. He'd tried to feed himself when Torrie became too ill to get out of her cot. He'd made his way into the hen house to look for eggs, but only succeeded in covering himself in chicken manure and feathers. As he couldn't heat water or wash his clothes, the stench still clung to him.

Despite the hunger gnawing at his belly, he fell into a fitful sleep. When he awoke he hardened his heart against his captive. He needed the boy's help to survive. Somehow he'd make it up to him.

Sydney estimated the shelter to be about ten feet wide and fifteen feet long. Shelves covered two adjacent walls. The third wall had two cots set against it, and the fourth wall was where she had started, where the stairs descended into the shelter.

She searched the shelves until she found a star-shaped tin candle holder. She dripped some hot wax onto it and pushed the candle firmly into the wax. It held. The small accomplishment made her feel more confident.

Under the bottom row of shelves sat one gallon and five gallon jugs. She tugged at one; they were filled with water. Two-thirds of the shelves were lined with jars of canned fruit and vegetables.

There were dishes, toilet paper, a hand-cranked weather radio, a pile of National Geographic and Hobby Farm magazines and a few books. She scanned the titles: *The Hobbit* by Tolkein, *A Search in Secret Egypt* by Paul Brunton, and three Martha Grimes mysteries.

She spied a white bucket with a lid in the corner next to the stairs. That had to be the toilet Jordan referred to. Sydney made use of it before she continued her search, but she turned up nothing more of interest. The shelter was equipped to hold two people for several weeks, or maybe a month at the most.

She set her pack on one of the cots and turned to scan the jars of canned goods. She may as well eat. She was hungry and she needed to keep up her strength. She pulled a jar of peaches off the shelf and found a can opener to pop the lid.

The smell of summer wafted into the storm cellar. She dipped her fingers into the jar, pulled out a slippery peach half, and popped the whole thing into her mouth. The peach was cool and silky smooth and sweet. Peach juice ran down her face and she groaned with the deliciousness of the fruit.

When the peaches were finished she poured a little water into a small bowl and cleaned her face and hands, then sat on the empty cot. She felt that she should do something, try to escape perhaps, but she was tired and she didn't see an obvious way out of the shelter other than the way she came in.

At least she was safe in her prison. No worries about travelers or hungry wild animals finding her while she slept. And it was fairly comfortable, much better than sleeping in the rough.

She could stay here for a few days, wait until Jordan released her, and then make her escape.

Sydney took off her boots and spread her sleeping bag on top of the cot, folded one blanket to use as a pillow, blew out the candle, and covered herself with the spare blanket. The cot felt luxurious after the nights she had spent sleeping on the ground, and she fell into a deep sleep.

Her nightmare returned more real than ever before. Barrett leered over her with his one eye, the other leaking blood that ran down his face. His hair and face were red and sticky with more blood. He bellowed at Sydney and threatened to kill her.

Sydney woke with a cry. She was drenched in sweat and tangled in the blanket. Where were the stars? Where was she?

She lay trembling in the cot until it all came rushing back to her. Jordan James, blind man, bereaved of his caretaker-sister, had imprisoned her in his storm cellar.

An almost palpable darkness enveloped her completely. Not even a pinpoint of light showed anywhere. It reminded her of a trip her family had made to Niagara Cave in Minnesota. The guide had switched off the lights to let the tourists experience the total blackness of a cave.

The difference then was that she had had a safety railing to hold on to and her parents standing on either side of her to keep her safe. Brave Shannon had tried to walk through the cave in the dark.

Her parents were gone. Shannon was gone. She had to rely on her own intelligence and strength to stay safe, to survive.

10

SYDNEY FLUNG the blanket to the side and swung her feet to the floor. She sat for a minute, listening for the tiniest sound, but she heard nothing. It was as if she was wearing the noise-canceling ear protectors she used while pistol shooting with her father. The silence felt unnatural.

Out in the world, no matter what the time of day or night, there was always something making noise: animals large and small, insects going about their business, the wind rustling leaves and grass or whining through the bare tree branches. Down in this hole in the ground there was nothing except silence and darkness.

A girl could go crazy down here alone.

Sydney groped for the candle holder that she had placed under the cot before going to sleep. She found it and pulled one of the matches she had pocketed from her pants, but it was damp from her sweat and wouldn't light. She oriented herself in the dark, trying to remember where the matches sat on the shelves, and stood.

With her hands in front of her, she took slow, careful steps across the floor until the candle holder dinged against a canning jar. The soft ting of the impact was swallowed up by the earthen space. The matches should be to her right, at the end of the shelf near the corner. She felt carefully along the shelf with her free hand, sidestepping one, two, three, four steps to her right until she located the match box.

She needed both hands to strike the match so she set the candle holder down. Operating in total darkness was incredibly difficult. Even star and moonlight provided enough light to maneuver by after dark.

She paused as she considered Jordan's life and how difficult it must be, how impossible for him to survive on his own. He didn't have the option of lighting a candle or fire to see by. Jordan lived in perpetual darkness, never knowing what surrounded him.

She pushed aside a sudden rush of pity for her captor.

After several tries she got the candle lit and turned to face her prison. She had to find a way out.

Holding the candle in front of her, Sydney paced off the space. Six steps wide by eight long. If her long steps were two and a half feet each then the cellar hole was approximately twelve feet by twenty feet.

She checked the two nooks on either side of the steps. The nook next to the stair wall held the white bathroom bucket and was used as the bathroom, the other nook held a stack of plastic totes.

Sydney set down the candle and pulled the top tote off the pile. She popped off the lid and was greeted with a musty smell. She checked the contents—it was filled with newspapers. Why would Jordan's family take up valuable space with newspapers?

She pulled one from the tote and spread it on the floor. It was yellowed and hard to read in the weak candlelight. She lowered herself to her hands and knees and scanned the page. A bold headline caught her eye.

"Local Boy Wins National Talent Contest."

Underneath the headline was a photo of Jordan James sitting at a piano and smiling. The paper was too yellowed and the candlelight too dim for her to read the piece. She pulled another paper from the box, and then another.

By reading the headlines and photo captions she deduced that before the world had been turned upside down, her captor had been a respected musician and singer. He had performed for the queen in England and the German chancellor and traveled to every continent to perform concerts.

She checked a date on a piece that noted his age and did the math. Jordan was in his mid twenties.

Sydney sat back on her heels. *How about that,* she thought with a wry smile, *I'm being held captive by a celebrity.* She put the papers back into the box and set it aside.

A quick look through the other boxes yielded more papers and sheet music with Jordan's name on them. He not only sang and played, he was also a composer. She felt another rush of sympathy for the man. It must have been difficult for him, losing his celebrity status.

"That doesn't give you the right to hold me prisoner!" she shouted up the stairs. There was no reply.

Sydney piled the totes back in their spot and returned to the cot. She blew out the candle and darkness enveloped her once more. She had no way of knowing what time of day or night it was.

The quiet pressed in on her and made her uncomfortable. She wrapped the blanket around her body and laid back down. Might as well try to rest while she could.

When she next woke she felt no confusion—she knew exactly where she was. She lay on the cot, listening for any indication that Jordan or Dogma were nearby, but she heard nothing.

She rolled onto her back and stared up into the inky blackness. This is what it's like to be blind. No matter how hard I try to see anything, I can't.

Her breathing and heartbeats were the only sounds in the storm cellar. Sydney's thoughts went to her grandfather, entombed in their cave, lying in the dark just as she was, his flesh slowly disintegrating from his bones.

She wondered if his flesh would rot or if he would desiccate and become mummy-like instead. Would she ever return to her family home and find out?

A single tear rolled down her temple and tickled her ear. She wiped it away and tried to force her thoughts to something else. What would Smokey do in her place? Smokey would thoroughly search the place and calmly assess the situation, she realized. She needed to do the same after she ate.

Sydney relit the candle, opened another jar of peaches, and ate the entire container standing in the middle of the storm cellar. While she ate she looked at the shelves, searching for items that could be used as weapons, or as tools to free herself.

She washed up and counted the candles. There were only six ten-inch tapers. She would need to conserve their use as there was no telling when Jordan would release her from this prison.

She found a rusted metal toolbox that held the essentials: a philips screwdriver, a small claw hammer, a handful of three-inch nails, electrical tape, wire cutters, and a slotted screwdriver that she pocketed. In a pinch it would make do as a weapon.

She also had her knives, slingshot, and pistol-sized crossbow in her backpack.

She noticed a small wooden tray of forks, spoons, and butter knives. She could hear her mother explaining that they were called flatware, chiding Sydney once when she incorrectly referred to them as silverware. Only utensils made from silver, or silver plate, were silverware, her mother corrected.

These were made from bone and stainless steel, not silver, therefor they were not silverware. Her mother had been a stickler for using the correct terminology to label things.

She found little else of interest on the shelves: a few plates, bowls, and cups, a couple of towels, the books and magazines. The remainder was taken up with canned goods, mostly peaches, plums, pickles, applesauce, and green beans.

Sydney sat back on the cot and blew out the candle. There was nothing to do but wait for Jordan to return. She slept and woke and slept, then lay on her back, eyes open with nothing to see. The storm cellar smelled of damp wood and earth, and the scent of peaches from her last meal still hung in the air. Gradually it dawned on her that there was a subtle difference in the darkness over in the corner with the totes.

She stood and carefully made her way toward them, her left arm outstretched to follow the wall over the cots, while her right arm searched the space in front of her. She walked by lifting one foot, moving it slowly in front of her, and setting it down. It was surprisingly difficult to keep her balance in the dark and she half-fell onto the cots twice.

When she reached the pile of totes she looked up. Dim light filtered through a narrow crack in the ceiling overhead. She realized that the floor of the outbuilding was the ceiling of the storm cellar.

She returned to her sleeping cot and felt underneath it for the candle. This time she was able to light it on her first try.

Sydney made her way back to the corner where she set the candleholder on a step while she rearranged the totes. She set two side by side and then placed two crossways on top of the first pair. She picked up the candleholder and set it on top of the second tier of totes and then tried to climb on top but the totes were too high. She grabbed the fifth tote and set it beside her construct and used it as a step.

She knelt carefully on the second level of totes. The lids gave way a bit, but then the papers they held provided support and she stopped sinking. She cautiously got to her feet and slowly stood up.

The totes wobbled beneath her and her head just missed a large oak beam that supported the outbuilding's floor. The candlelight drowned out the light that had been filtering through the floor boards. Sydney held it as close as she dared to the wood above her and looked for cracks.

She pulled the screwdriver from her pocket and tried to fit the point between two boards with no success. She then tried to jab the sharp end of the screwdriver into a floor board. It bounced off, barely leaving a mark.

"Darn oak." Early settlers had favored the abundant oak for constructing the old post and beam barns and outbuildings found in the midwest. A hard wood to begin with, over the centuries the tightly grained oak beams shrunk and hardened even further, until it became impossible to even drive a nail into them.

Sydney crawled down off the totes and put them back in the corner. She crept up the steps and felt for the edges of the trapdoor with her fingers. It too was made from oak and the hinges were on the outside.

She blew out the candle and waited on the steps for what felt like several hours, but Jordan still did not return.

Time lost all meaning for Sydney. She slept, she ate fruit and pickles, she spent long stretches of time sitting on the steps waiting for Jordan's return, and she slept again.

Her nightmares became more frequent and she often awoke with tears on her face. She dreamed of Shannon's murder. She dreamed that her grandfather tried to stand but couldn't because he was trapped in the rug she had rolled around his body.

Mostly she dreamed about Cal and Barrett and their desire to chase her down and avenge their own murders.

Bored with sleeping and afraid to dream, Sydney decided to burn a candle and read. She had read *The Hobbit* as a child so she passed that up and chose *A Search in Secret Egypt* instead.

She became so engrossed in the author's recounting of his journey through Egypt and his overnight stay alone inside the Great Pyramid, that she never heard the footsteps over her head until Jordan called to her.

"Hey, Sydney Waters, you still in there?" She heard a humorless chuckle. "Of course you are, where else would you be?"

Sydney grabbed the candleholder and climbed the steps. "Jordan! Are you ready to let me out of here?" She sensed the man and his dog standing on the other side of the trapdoor.

"Well now, that depends. Have you had time to think about my offer?"

Sydney took a deep breath and let it out in a long sigh. Apparently she would not be let out until she agreed to be Jordan's new caretaker. She had been raised not to lie, but her world had changed—perhaps now was a good time to start practicing.

"Is this how you persuaded your sister to take care of you?" she asked. There was silence over her head and Sydney wondered if she had pissed Jordan off. Too bad. He had no right to treat her this way.

"No," came the reply after a few moments. "Torrie was happy to be a part of my life. She did everything for me, even traveled with me when I performed. Did you find the newspapers?"

"Yeah, I saw them. Doesn't matter how great a musician you are, you can't lock people up just because you want something from them."

"That's where you're wrong, Waters. I can and I have. Apparently you haven't been locked up long enough. You need more time to think. Good-bye."

"Wait! Jordan! You can't leave yet, let me out of here!" She pounded on the trapdoor with her fist but Jordan and Dogma had already gone.

11

"CRAP."

Sydney scrambled down the steps and grabbed the toolbox. She brought it back up the steps and pulled out the screwdriver and hammer. She tried to envision which side of the trapdoor held the hinges.

She thought she remembered the trapdoor sitting to the left side of the hole when it was open. That meant that they were on her right as she faced the top step.

She stuck the tip of the screwdriver into the edge of the door and tapped it with the hammer. It took several taps to drive the shaft into the narrow space until the handle stopped its progress. She'd missed the hinge.

She patiently worked the screwdriver free and tried another spot an inch farther along the door's edge. Missed the hinge again.

On her fifth try Sydney felt resistance. Her pulse quickened and she tapped the screwdriver as hard as she could. It didn't move. She hit it hard several times until the plastic handle split apart in her hand.

She wrestled the shaft out of the crack and wrapped the handle with electrical tape. She knew that she was wasting her time. Her small screwdriver was no match for the large and sturdy hinges that held the heavy door.

She shifted to the opposite side of the trapdoor and started again, looking for the hasp that held the door shut. This time she had better luck. She found the hasp on her third attempt and loosened it with only two strikes.

She heard a faint thunk as the metal flange of the hasp popped up and hit the door. Excited now and tasting victory, Sydney pushed against the door. It didn't yield even a fraction of an inch.

She crawled one step higher and positioned her back against the door. Her hamstrings cramped, forcing her to descend and stretch until the cramps receded.

She crawled back up the steps and tried a third time, putting all her strength into her push. Her thighs quivered with the effort but the door still did not move.

She sat on a step, stretched her legs out again to relieve the cramps, and thought about the problem. She should be able to lift the trapdoor—no one would design a storm cellar that trapped its occupants inside. Jordan must have placed something heavy on top of the door to ensure that she couldn't escape.

Defeated, she sat on the steps for a long while. Her candle stub burned down and sputtered out. She climbed down the steps and walked to the cot. It was getting easier for her to navigate her prison without lighting a candle.

She was beginning to understand how Jordan navigated through his life of darkness. Her sense of hearing and smell had grown sharper just in the time she had been trapped in the storm cellar. How much better would they be if she had to rely on them all the time?

Time stretched as she waited. She had no idea how long she'd been a prisoner. It felt as if days had passed. She didn't bother to light the candle. Instead she felt her way around, ate when she was hungry, used the bucket, and lay on the cot and waited for Jordan's return.

When she heard him overhead again she was ready for him.

"Jordan! What do I have to do to get out of here?"

The footsteps stopped. "You have to care for the chickens: feed them, gather their eggs, and clean the coop. You also have to work the garden and preserve what you grow, as well as get water from the well and gather firewood and cook. I can take care of my personal needs but I need help with the other stuff. Dogma hunts and feeds herself. Why? Are you ready to agree to those terms?"

Sydney gritted her teeth. She had no intention of sticking around to be Jordan James's personal attendant, but agreeing seemed to be the only way out of the storm cellar. She would sneak off sometime when Dogma was off hunting or busy with Jordan.

"Yes, yes, I agree. Now let me out of here."

"Great."

Sydney detected a note of relief in Jordan's voice. It occurred to her that getting by on his own while she was held captive had been difficult for him. She pushed away the spurt of compassion she felt. *The man had imprisoned her. He didn't deserve her pity.*

She heard a squeak, and then the trapdoor started moving. She ran down the steps and grabbed her pack and sleeping bag. Sunlight flooded the opening and she closed her eyes against the brightness of it, blinking them open and closed a few times until her pupils adjusted to the light.

Sydney climbed out of the storm cellar and looked at

Jordan with curiosity. It had been too dark to make out his features the night he had trapped her.

She saw a handsome man with no visible sign of his affliction. Large gray eyes, marred only by the bruised, delicate shadows underneath, looked straight at her as if they were seeing her.

His light brown hair was tied back from his strong face in a short ponytail. He sported a bump in his otherwise straight nose and had an attractive mouth. She sniffed. He needed a bath.

Dogma stood at Jordan's side, her golden eyes intent upon Sydney's face as if she were assessing Sydney's reaction to her master.

"First thing you need to take care of is the chickens," said Jordan. "They need to be fed and watered and any eggs collected. I'll show you where the coop is." He turned away from her and took several steps, then folded up like an abandoned marionette.

"Jordan? What's wrong? Jordan, can you hear me?"

Sydney set down her pack and rushed to Jordan's body. She was relieved to find that his breathing seemed normal, but his pulse was irregular. She noted his thin, bony wrists, and sunken cheeks. As she adjusted his body to a more comfortable position she realized that he was severely undernourished.

"So, how long have you been going without food, I wonder?"

Dogma whined and laid down next to her master, one of her large paws on Jordan's arm.

Sydney went back to the storm cellar. She hesitated at the head of the steps. *I really don't want to go back down there.* She waffled a moment, then ran down and grabbed two blankets and several jars of peaches.

She placed a folded blanket under Jordan's head and spread the other one over his body. She set the peaches on the ground near him and went to find the chicken coop. She needed to get some food into her captor and fresh eggs were a good source of fat and protein.

She remembered hearing chickens as Jordan led her to the storm cellar the night he had captured her. She turned in the direction of the large cottonwood on the opposite side of the yard to retrace her steps.

The smell of a dirty coop reached her well before she heard the cackle of hens. She opened the coop door and the pungent smell of ammonia rolled out and washed over her.

She braced the door open with a chunk of wood, stood to the side, and waited. Moments later a pair of reddish brown hens came clucking out the door. They flew a few feet and started scratching for insects. Four more hens joined the first two.

Sydney stuck her head inside the coop. The ammonia made her eyes sting and she drew back. She trotted back to her pack and dug out a bandana, tied it over her mouth and nose, and then entered the coop.

There were three more hens left inside. She shooed them out into the fresh air and sunshine, then rooted around the nest boxes for eggs. She found several dozen but could only carry six. She decided to come back later with a container for the rest.

She was relieved to see Jordan sitting up when she returned to him, a sheepish expression on his face. Sydney carefully set down the eggs and opened a jar of peaches. She placed it in his hands along with a spoon.

"Eat these, they'll help fill your belly while I put together a fire for cooking."

Jordan's face lit up when he smelled the peaches. Ignoring

the spoon he dug a dirty finger into the jar and popped one into his mouth. Peach juice ran down his hand and face and dripped onto his tee shirt.

"Mmm, gawd these are good. Torrie always did right by our peach tree." He ate a few more, set the jar down carefully, and kept his hand on it as if afraid they'd disappear if he let go.

"You don't need a cooking fire," he said. "The gas stove works. We have two large propane tanks and Torrie is…I mean was…stingy with her use of it. She turned off the hot water heater so the gas would last longer for cooking. She was smart that way, always thinking ahead and figuring out ways for us to get by."

Sydney had questions, but they could wait. She gathered up the eggs and headed toward the house. "I'll get these eggs boiling and come back for you," she said over her shoulder.

The back door led directly into the kitchen but Sydney did not go straight in. She set the eggs on the steps and walked around the house first.

The windows were boarded over with plywood from the inside. Many of them held jagged pieces of glass: broken by vandals or from the earthquakes, she couldn't tell. She wondered if they had been boarded over before or after they were broken.

Trash and debris littered the lawn and the front porch and much of the house paint was flaking or gone altogether. Several upholstered chairs and a couch lay on their sides on the lawn. Loose stuffing poked through their once fine covers.

The house looked abandoned. Sydney breathed a little easier. Travelers would be less likely to bother with a place that had already been ransacked, and the James house looked as if it had been cleaned out.

She returned to the rear of the house, picked up the eggs, and entered the kitchen. The kitchen windows were also boarded over, but whoever had done it had left several inches free at the top so enough light filtered in to see by.

Sydney rummaged through the cabinets until she found a sauce pan. No water flowed from the faucet but she found several five gallon jugs lined up side by side on a counter. Three were empty, the fourth one she tried yielded enough for the eggs. She made a mental note to ask Jordan how Torrie refilled the jugs.

While the eggs cooked Sydney explored the rest of the house. Larger than her grandfather's modest place, Jordan's house would have once been considered a "show place." There were tattered remains of once fine drapes and carpets, and broken chandeliers hanging by their wires in the two front rooms.

She walked through five bedrooms and three bathrooms. Dust and cobwebs covered every surface. Apparently Torrie had wasted no energy trying to keep these rooms clean. Not that Sydney blamed her—what was the point? Obviously no one used these rooms.

She found a Steinway Baby Grand piano in the front parlor. Someone had pried off the ivory keys and several deep scratches ran across the top. It made her feel sad to see such a beautiful instrument destroyed.

Sydney resisted the impulse to press the piano's remaining keys; her intuition told her that the sound would upset Jordan. The piano obviously belonged to him, and she suspected he wouldn't like other people touching it.

Two walls of the parlor were covered with floor to ceiling shelves that contained part of what was once Jordan's vast collection of trophies. The remaining two walls held framed awards and photos of him playing: Carnegie Hall in New

York City, the restored Orpheum Theater in Minneapolis, the Grand Old Opry in Nashville. Venues in Europe and Australia. An autographed photo of Jordan standing between the king and queen of Denmark.

Sydney finished her tour of the house and returned to the eggs. She gave Torrie credit for making the kitchen livable. A large country style kitchen with an abundance of cabinets and shelving, Jordan's sister had made one corner the sleeping area, setting two narrow cots at right angles to each other.

Two photos hung on the wall over the cots: one showed an attractive brunette jumping a horse in a show ring, the other was a photo of a young Jordan James in a baseball uniform, a wide smile on his already handsome face. A hank of thick, tawny hair fell over one eye, giving him a roguish look.

Sydney stared at the photos for several minutes. Jordan and Torrie had been a normal American brother and sister from a somewhat privileged background. A lump grew in her chest, a deep yearning for the days before The Upheaval.

She turned away from the photos but then spun back—if Jordan had played baseball then he had not been born blind. Something had robbed him of his sight.

She found a bowl to pour the boiling egg water into and set the eggs on the table to cool. After adding a little water from the jug to bring down the temperature of the hot water she washed her face and hands, then quickly stripped down and took a fast sponge bath.

The warm water felt heavenly and getting rid of some of the dusty grime that coated her body boosted her morale. She rinsed out her underwear, hung it on the towel rack and redressed. She'd change into clean clothes when she could get to her pack and then she'd wash out her dirty clothes. The prospect of clean clothes cheered her immensely.

"I SAW some of your trophies and awards," Sydney said later, after she and Jordan had polished off a second batch of eggs. Even Dogma received a couple, taking them with great delicacy from Jordan's fingers.

Sydney sat at the kitchen table while Jordan sat cross-legged on his cot, rocking to and fro, a slight motion that Sydney guessed was nervous habit.

Jordan gave a slight nod. "Yeah, that all happened in another lifetime. I haven't touched the Baby in a couple years now. The risk's too great that someone will hear it."

"You must miss playing." She didn't tell him that his Baby was missing most of her keys.

Jordan shrugged. "It's the one thing I can still do well. It made me feel useful. The money I made helped to pay back the medical bills and supported us."

Here was the opening she needed to learn more. "Speaking of medical bills, you weren't always blind, were you? I found a photo of you playing baseball when you were young."

Jordan pressed his lips together and shook his head.

Sydney waited. Jordan added nothing more. "Did you have an illness?" she prompted.

"No." He gave a heavy sigh. "My parents were driving me home from a baseball game one Saturday afternoon and a drunk ran a stop sign and t-boned our car. I was banged up and suffered a brain injury. The specialist said that the part of my brain that interpreted the impulses from my optic nerves was damaged, and by the time I left the hospital I was blind."

"Ouch, that must have been so hard for you. What did your parents do? Did they look for someone to try surgery?"

"No. Both of my parents died in the accident." Jordan's tone was curt. He obviously didn't want to talk about it but Sydney couldn't let it go.

"And?"

"And what?" asked Jordan, scowling.

"And then what happened?" asked Sydney, refusing to be cowed. For a long moment Jordan said nothing and she thought he was going to ignore her, but then he sighed.

"My sister Torrie was living in New York City at the time, working at an ad agency. She set aside her life to come back here and take care of me. I'd rather not talk about it anymore if you don't mind."

They sat in silence for several minutes. Sydney was glad to see that some color had returned to Jordan's face. He had revived considerably with food in his belly. Dogma sat close by his side. She stared at Sydney with bright golden colored eyes.

"What does Dogma eat?" she asked. "Should I feed her something more? A couple eggs doesn't seem like enough for such a large dog."

"Dogma hunts when she's hungry, but you can give her some more of the raw eggs if you want."

Sydney found a plastic bowl, scrambled a couple eggs in it, and set the bowl on the floor near the huge dog. Dogma ignored the eggs. One ear perked up as though she were waiting for a command.

"It's okay, Dogma, eat," said Jordan. The dog stood and padded over to the bowl.

Sydney was astonished by how delicately she lapped up the eggs. When Dogma had licked the bowl clean she returned to Jordan's side. "She sure is an impressive beast. Did you name her?"

Jordan buried a hand in Dogma's thick, wiry coat and a wistful smile passed over his face. "Naw, that was Torrie. She was a bit of a rebel, always questioning authority and rules. Dogma was more her dog than mine, but Torrie told her to watch over me and she sticks with me. She seems to understand most of what she hears."

Sydney looked at the dog with curiosity. Dogma's wise eyes stared back at Sydney and she had the intense feeling that Dogma did indeed understand what was going on around her.

"I can't take your sister's place, you know. I have to find my friend. But I can't leave you here to starve to death either. It's obvious that you can't fend for yourself."

Sydney gathered the dirty dishes and set them in a plastic dish pan. "I've been thinking about what to do and I think it's best if you come with me. We'll find a functioning town or community where there will be people who can look after you."

Jordan's rocking stopped and the color drained from his face. "I can't do that. I can't leave the farm. I-I can't survive out there on my own, not without Torrie to help me."

"Nonsense," said Sydney. "You've been all over the world, I saw the photos. It will be a challenge, I agree, but you'll learn to cope, and you'll have Dogma to watch over you. I promise I won't leave you unless I know you'll be safe. You can't stay here alone, you'll die."

Jordan's fingers began to move against his pant legs. Sydney watched them for a moment, puzzled, and then realized they mimed playing the piano. His mouth was pressed tight and his brow wrinkled. He rocked and played for several minutes and then stopped abruptly. "If you try to leave I'll order Dogma to attack," he said, his voice hard and cold.

Shocked by his threat, Sydney could only stare at Jordan. Her temper flared but she quickly doused it. Jordan had to be frightened now that his sister was no longer at his side, she reminded herself. He was only doing what he felt he had to do in order to survive.

Survival was difficult enough in this new world. To survive while handicapped with the loss of one's sight was near impossible. The man had a right to utter threats.

"Then you will starve to death here," she answered mildly, "because I refuse to be held as a slave and I will not care for you. Dogma may be able to stop me from leaving, but she can't force me to feed you. I'll help you my way or not at all."

Sydney wiped her hands and left the house. The sun was shining, a welcome contrast to the dim kitchen and the dark storm cellar. She sat on the back steps, lifted her face to the sky, and soaked up the warm rays while she waited to see what the piano man would do next.

An hour passed and there was no sign of Jordan. Sydney opened the back door a crack and peered in. He was asleep on his cot, mouth slightly open and softly snoring. Dogma lay at his side, her eyes on Sydney.

Sydney closed the door and considered her options. Now was her chance to escape—with Dogma closed inside the house and Jordan asleep she could be miles up the road before he even realized she had gone.

She didn't owe Jordan James anything. His life was not her responsibility.

She grabbed her pack and headed down the drive, happy to be moving again. It felt good to be walking in the bright sunshine. She wasn't sure, but she guessed that she had lost the better part of a week trapped down in Jordan's storm cellar.

Halfway to the gravel road her steps slowed until she stood unmoving. The sun was still shining, crows called in the distance, the road still beckoned her, but Sydney stood frozen in her tracks.

She couldn't leave a helpless man to starve to death. She already had the deaths of two men and Shannon on her conscience and she couldn't bear to add another. Besides, she had forgotten to retrieve her clean underwear.

There had to be a way to persuade Jordan to join her. She could look for an appropriate place to leave him where he would be fed and safe. Or at least as safe as anyone could be these days.

She sighed and turned back toward the house. "Might as well clean out the chicken coop."

13

JORDAN SLEPT for most of the day. While he slept, Sydney explored the farm. She found the wind-powered well and washed her dirty clothes, thankful that she hadn't changed into clean ones before tackling the filthy chicken coop. She brought up more canned goods from the storm cellar and piled them off to the side of the kitchen door so Jordan wouldn't step on them if he came outside.

The James farm had been lovely at one time. Flower beds, now overrun with weeds, dotted the grounds, and she found a large vegetable garden beside the smaller barn. Bees were busy gathering pollen before the cold weather set in and phoebes and barn swallows darted after insects. A fruit orchard held a variety of trees that Sydney couldn't identify. She bit into an apple but it wasn't quite ready. It puckered her mouth and she spit it out.

She was surprised to find a pony behind the abandoned cow barn. It lived in a large fenced pasture with a small stream running across the back end. Even more surprising, the pony looked well-nourished and healthy.

It walked right up to Sydney and sniffed her apple-scented hand. She ducked low to check the pony's gender and then rubbed its dark brown nose. The little mare stretched her head closer. Sydney climbed through the fence to scratch her back and neck. The mare accepted her scratches before wandering off to graze.

Sydney watched her for a few minutes, thinking of ways to put her to use. A pack animal would make it much easier for Jordan to travel. A plan began to form in her mind. It would take a week or longer to prepare, but that was okay— it wasn't as if Smokey was expecting her. She felt lighter and more hopeful as she finished her exploration of the farm.

When she circled back to the henhouse later she trapped an older bird. There would be chicken soup for dinner tonight.

"Is that your sister's pony behind the barn?" Sydney and Jordan had just finished eating several bowls of her chicken soup. She had discovered potatoes and carrots in the garden and added them to the soup. She eyed Jordan with approval as he ate, happy to see that he had a healthy appetite.

Jordan slurped up the last bit of broth from his bowl and set it on the table. "Sort of. That's Kria. Torrie bought Kria for me to ride, but she spent more time with her than I did. Torrie always related better to animals than to people. I think Kria was as dear to her as me and Dogma were. I should probably go visit her and tell her about Torrie. "

"Can you ride?"

Jordan looked surprised by the question. He shrugged. "I used to ride. I haven't been on her in a while, but sure, I can ride. Why?"

"I'm thinking we should take Kria with us. If you ride and

I lead her it will make traveling easier. When we get to some-place where you can stay we can sell or trade her to help pay for your care."

Jordan frowned and shook his head. "Kria is family. I can't sell her."

"We'll need-" Sydney stopped. There would be time later for this argument. She would simply deal with Kria when the proper time came. "I understand how you feel. Have you had enough to eat? I'm going to clean up," she said instead.

———

Sydney quickly slipped into a daily routine on the James farm. She let the chickens out to forage and gathered their eggs first thing in the morning, after which she and Jordan shared some of Torrie's canned fruit for breakfast.

She then worked on preparations for their journey. She gathered and washed Jordan's dirty clothes and set aside the ones that were suitable for travel. She cleaned the accumu-lated junk out of the smoke house and readied it for use.

She also began to spend time with Kria, getting to know the little mare. More important, she wanted Kria to become comfortable with her. She looked good for a pony Jordan had told her was well into her twenties.

With her broad, flat back and thick neck, Kria had the typical stocky build of one of the tough Icelandic breeds. Her pale brown coat and dark chestnut head gave her the appear-ance that she wore a hood. Her thick mane stood straight and stiff like a bottle brush, a blend of pale brown flecked with black and white hairs.

Sydney rubbed Kria's soft muzzle and picked thistle heads to hand feed her. The mare sniffed them and then deli-cately plucked them from Sydney's open palm.

One afternoon, after grooming Kria and finding her treats, Sydney rummaged through the barns until she came up with some pieces of tack: a leather halter and lead line and a suede bareback pad. She didn't find any saddles; they had likely been stolen.

She found a pony cart but no rigging so she dismissed it. More digging produced a long coil of two inch webbing. She inspected her finds. Unless he rode bareback, it looked like Jordan would have to walk after all, but at least Kria could carry his belongings.

Later that evening after they had eaten, Sydney outlined her plan to Jordan. She took it as a positive sign when he didn't argue, and felt grateful that he had come to accept that he couldn't remain in his home any longer. It would make her task much easier if he didn't fight her all the way.

The next day Sydney slaughtered all but two of the chickens, cleaned and boned them, and prepped them for the smokehouse. She had already collected her green wood from the orchard, culling limbs and spouts from the apple trees. The chickens would take on the sweetness from the applewood smoke as they cured, a trick her grandfather had taught her. Although dry, they'd taste delicious.

She found two duffle bags in one of the upstairs closets and used one to hold Jordan's spare clothing along with several blankets. He didn't own a sleeping bag and that concerned her, but there was nothing she could do about it.

While the chickens smoked, Sydney spent an entire day building two small, lightweight cages from flexible green branches for the remaining two hens. She rigged the cages so they swung off a short pole that she lashed to the top of her pack, imitating a photo she had seen of peasant farmers carrying their fowl to market.

She added a spool of cotton kitchen twine to an outside

pocket in her pack; with it she could tether the hens so they would be able to search for insects and greens to feed themselves. She hoped the setup would work well enough to keep the birds alive. Fresh eggs would help feed her and Jordan on their journey.

While Sydney's days were filled with preparations, Jordan filled her evenings with stories of his travels. He appeared to accept the need to leave his home and he became friendlier toward her. He amazed her with his powers of observation. Despite his blindness, it seemed very little escaped his notice.

He possessed an amazing memory for smells and sounds and for overheard conversations. He also possessed a knack for mimicry and made her laugh with his foolish impersonations.

Five days passed. The butchered chickens finished smoking. Sydney was pleased with how well they turned out. The meat was slightly shrunken and golden brown and smelled of sweet applewood. She scrounged a plastic lidded container from the kitchen cupboards and packed the meat into it.

Sydney went through her mental checklist. The preparations were complete. Tomorrow she would lead a blind man, a giant dog, two chickens and a pony into the unknown.

The daring of her undertaking made her nervous, but she also recognized a feeling of excitement underneath her uncertainty. She realized that was looking forward to the challenge and the knowledge brought a small smile to her face. Shannon would be proud of her twin sister.

14

The next morning dawned clear and cool. Sydney let the two remaining hens out to forage while she boiled the remaining eggs. They shared two jars of peaches for breakfast and packed the eggs into the cooking pots for lunch later in the day.

She filled the water containers, brought Kria out of her pasture and placed the bareback pad on her, then lashed Jordan's bag of clothes to one side and the blanket bag to the opposite side. She checked that they hung evenly, added the two filled water jugs, one to a side to keep the load balanced, and tied Kria to the fence rail. She scooped up the hens and secured them in their carry cages, then lashed the cages to her pack.

"Jordan! Jordan! Let's go! We're burning daylight." She waited several minutes but Jordan didn't appear.

Feeling a little annoyed, Sydney entered the house. Jordan wasn't in the kitchen so she walked deeper into the building. She heard a tiny 'plink' and headed for the parlor. Jordan stood at the piano, running his fingers lightly up and down the ruined keys. His lips moved but no words came out.

"Are you ready?" Sydney asked, her voice soft. "I know this is hard for you, leaving everything you know behind, and I imagine it's scary as well, but we have to leave. I don't know any way to make it easier for you, except to say that Dogma and Kria will be with you."

Jordan hung his head, but not before Sydney saw the shine of tears in his eyes. She walked up to him and took his hand and tugged gently. He offered no resistance and let her lead him from the house. As if sensing his distress, Dogma pressed close to his side.

Once outdoors she helped Jordan don the small backpack she had found and filled with a few of his things. She handed him her grandfather's walking stick.

"What's this?" he asked, his fingers running over the stick's carved surface. He traced the ram horns and smiled. "A shepherd's staff?"

"It was my grandfather's walking stick. I carved it for his birthday a couple of years ago. It's ironwood." She hesitated as the image of her grandfather trying to save her from Barrett flashed in her mind. "He-he really loved that stick. It's sturdy enough to use as a weapon if you ever need one."

She put on her own pack, careful not to bang the chicken's cages against anything. They squawked and then settled down. She untied Kria's lead and the procession headed awkwardly down the drive.

Jordan bumped into Sydney several times as he struggled to walk a straight line. His face reddened and he mumbled an apology each time.

Sydney sensed his humility and frustration and wisely kept her mouth shut. Walking in the open was a new skill that he would master. She moved to Jordan's left side, placing Dogma between them. Dogma kept her body pressed against Jordan and his path grew straighter.

As they put distance between themselves and the James farm Jordan relaxed. His stride became less tentative and more sure. He used the walking stick but did not tap it in front of him the way Sydney had seen sightless people use their canes. His free hand rested lightly on Dogma's head and that seemed to be enough guidance for him.

Sydney began to breath easier and let loose some of the tension she had been holding inside. She lengthened her stride a little and everyone kept up. Good. She didn't know if she was doing the right thing, taking Jordan away from all that he knew, but she was positive that she didn't want to spend the remainder of her life on his farm caring for him.

The morning passed without any major troubles. They stopped and sat in the shade of a large willow to lunch and rest. Sydney released the chickens and tied their tethers to a nearby sapling. The birds scooted about after insects and the occasional green shoot, all the while clucking contentedly.

Kria grazed on whatever she could find. Jordan was quiet, but he ate the eggs that Sydney handed to him and obediently changed his socks when she explained how important it was to keep his feet dry.

Unused to walking any distance, Jordan moved more slowly as the day wore on, but he never complained.

Sydney's respect for the blind piano player grew. How would she behave in similar circumstances? She liked to think that she would be fearless and face whatever came her way with confidence, but she truly didn't know if she could overcome such a serious physical handicap.

She closed her eyes for a minute and imagined she was blind. She immediately stumbled and her steps grew small and tentative. And that was knowing the road lay straight in front of her, she thought with disgust. Jordan has no idea what lay around him.

She suddenly understood the trust that Jordan had placed in her and felt a moment of panic. What if she let him down the same way she had let Shannon and her grandfather down? What right did she have to demand that Jordan trust her?

Sydney shook off her panic and focused on their immediate needs. Her biggest worry now was running into other travelers. It had been relatively simple to hide when she traveled alone. Now she was part of a larger, much more noticeable group, and an easy target for robbery. Kria and the chickens would provide a fair amount of meat to a starving family, and Jordan and Sydney's clothes and boots could be stolen right off their bodies. Alive or dead.

She fretted about their safety until she recalled a conversation she'd once had with Smokey as they practiced the Slow Walk along the river.

She remembered how beautiful the Mississippi had shone that day, reflecting sunlight like a million fractured stars dancing on the river's surface. It had been a warm, soft spring day, with small flocks of ducks and geese traveling up the river, calling to one another in the eons-old songs of spring. Sydney's mind had been occupied with other things, things she had no control over, just like now.

"Sydney! Where is your focus?" Smokey had asked her, after she had stepped on and broken yet another dry stick. She admitted that her thoughts were miles away, fretting about whether her father would return from his latest business trip before she went to bed that night.

Smokey had stopped and faced her. "Can you do anything at this moment to help your father's travels?"

Sydney shook her head. "No."

"Is he here with you now?"

"No."

"Then you must focus your attention on what you can affect, which is only what you are doing at the moment. Your father may or may not make it home tonight, that is not up to you. You will deal with whatever happens when the time comes."

Sydney had argued that she was only being a loving daughter, concerned about her father's welfare.

"Ah," said Smokey, "so you believe that by fretting, you will help your father get home? It is just the opposite, Syd. If you truly love your father you will imagine him healthy and happy. Nothing more, nothing less. Our thoughts have power, much more power than people realize. Do not send negative thoughts his way, or surround your own being with negative energy."

Learning the Slow Walk had been a life-changing challenge for Sydney. It took great focus, fortitude, and self-discipline, far more than she had thought she possessed.

And yet every time she was sure that she had had enough, she dug deeper into her being and discovered that she was unable to quit, that she had to keep striving for excellence. The longer she worked for it, the more she understood that perfection was a never-ending quest.

"Jordan, how did you know I was standing by the tree that first night?"

"I felt you there," came the answer.

"The wind was blowing from you to me. Even Dogma couldn't smell me and I wasn't moving or making any noise."

Jordan shrugged. "I don't know how I knew. It's as if I developed some sort of personal radar after I went blind. It works with inanimate objects too, only not quite as well. I just sense that something is occupying space. I felt an extra presence by the tree that I knew shouldn't be there."

They walked several miles in comfortable silence. The

hens had settled into their cages after their midday forage, and the four-beat clip-clop of Kria's hooves sounding out their pace like an equine metronome, was soothing.

"How close does someone or something have to be to you before you pick it up?"

"I don't know. I can't see them to judge distances. Why?"

"I'm not sure. I've been thinking that we could be an attractive target for the Desperate Ones, especially the closer we get to any towns. I'm wondering if we should start traveling at night and lay low during the daylight hours. You and Dogma and Kria won't have any trouble walking in the dark, and I'm sure I could get the hang of it quick enough."

Jordan turned his head toward Sydney, his brows furrowed. Today his gray eyes reminded her of smoky mirrors. If she didn't know that he was blind, she'd swear he was looking at her. His eyes seemed to look deep inside her.

"What kind of trouble? Who are the Desperate Ones?" he asked.

"Well–," she hesitated. "You must know there are people who have lost everything. They look for stuff to trade for food. They could steal our supplies. Or Kria. They might even…eat her."

Jordan walked in silence while he digested this. "And?"

"How do you know there's an 'and'"? asked Sydney.

"I hear it in your voice. You're worried about something more."

Sydney swallowed. She didn't want to say the words aloud, didn't want to give her thoughts any more power than they already had. But Jordan deserved to know the dangers they faced.

"There are monsters out here who rape and kill for pleasure," she whispered.

They walked another mile before Jordan replied. "Let's

travel at night when we get near any towns. Do you have maps so we know where we are?"

"I have the maps I need to find my friend Smokey. My plan was to cross Iowa and take you to Vermillion, South Dakota. It's not too large, only fifteen thousand people or so, so hopefully it fared better than the larger places, like Sioux City or Des Moines. The travelers who stopped by my family's farm told us that the larger the city, the worse the devastation. Smaller towns tend to be more self-sufficient so they mostly escaped the looting and riots, although there are always men who will take advantage and steal from others."

Wrinkles appeared on Jordan's brow. "Have you had any experience with these Desperate Ones?"

"Yes." Sydney refused to say anymore about it. She didn't feel ready to share what she had witnessed and done, especially with a man who had lived a golden, protected life. She wasn't even sure she could confess to Smokey that she had murdered two men.

She decided to change the subject. "Where were you when everything changed?"

"Torrie and I had just returned from a concert series in Chile. She set Kria loose and we headed into the storm shelter. It was a little scary being underground during the earthquakes, but we survived."

"We were lucky too. We lost a couple small buildings that weren't too sturdy to begin with, but that was the worst of it for us. Besides losing my parents that is."

Sydney told Jordan about her mother's art show and the tsunamis that wiped out the east coast.

"My sister Torrie had a theory. She believed that the earth is a living entity with a consciousness. Different from us, but still conscious. She said the earth got fed up with the way man was treating her: sucking all the underground reservoirs dry of oil and coal and water until the surface land collapsed."

"Your sister sounds like an interesting woman."

"Yeah, she could get pretty radical sometimes. Anyway, she believed the earth was fighting back in the only way possible—by unleashing natural disasters." He shrugged. "There's no way to prove it of course."

15

THEY FOUND a small barn to spend the night in. One half of it had collapsed in on itself, but the other side seemed sturdy and was dry.

Sydney removed Kria's load and rubbed her down, then hobbled her before setting her loose to forage in the pasture behind the barn. She tied the chickens out with the pony and then searched the farm for any fresh edibles to eat with their smoked chicken.

She was thrilled to discover a patch of first year Queen Anne's Lace. Once considered a pesky weed by most farmers, it was a wild carrot treat for Sydney. She dug a dozen of them with the narrow forked tool she had taken from the James farm. She also found a half-full rain barrel set under a downspout and after cleaning the wild carrots she filled a pot with water for a quick soup.

The barn had a packed dirt floor, and after she removed some flammable debris Sydney felt it was safe to build a small cooking fire inside. She scrounged dead limbs and scrap barn boards for fuel, opened the doors at both ends of the building to give the smoke a place to vent, and soon had a fire crackling.

When dinner was finished she dowsed the fire and fluffed some loose hay she'd found into two piles. She placed Jordan's blankets on one and rolled up in her sleeping bag on the other. She fell asleep as soon as she closed her eyes.

"Sid. Sidney, wake up." A hand gripped her shoulder.

"Go away. I'm sleeping."

"Sid!" Jordan's whisper was insistent. "There's someone outside the barn."

Sydney scrambled from her sleeping bag, wide awake. "How do you know?"

Jordan knelt beside her, his hand on her arm. "I heard voices," he whispered. "They're in the yard, on the other side of the house."

"How many?" Sydney mentally kicked herself. She had let down her guard and broken her first rule of life on the road: never get trapped in a building by other travelers.

"I'm not sure. I heard two men and a woman."

"You wait here. Keep Dogma with you. Keep quiet. I'm going to get closer to check them out."

A woman could mean they were innocent travelers like Sydney and Jordan, but Sydney also knew that the women travelers could be as ruthless as any man, or even worse. It occurred to her that if they were good people they might be willing to take Jordan with them, and she could be on her way to find Smokey. He would be safer traveling with a larger party, especially if it included men for protection.

She didn't take the time to put on her boots. Barefoot would be quieter. She glided to the barn door and stood to the side listening. She could hear the voices now, over by the back door of the house, but it was too dark to see them. There had been only a sliver of moon tonight and it had already set. She would have to get closer if she was going to learn anything.

She took several steps outside the barn, using its bulk for cover. She stopped and waited, but the newcomers didn't seem to be aware of her so she walked silently to the corner of the barn nearest the house and waited again.

"She's slowing us down. I say we leave her here." The voice was gruff. It sounded as if it belonged to an older man.

"I can keep up. I didn't slow you down today." A woman. Sydney cringed at the whining tone in her voice. Whining and begging were signs of weakness. If the woman's companions were bad people they would take advantage of that weakness.

"Do you have money, or anything of value to pay us for helping you?" A second man. His voice was hard and reminded Sydney of Cal and Barrett. She took several steps closer and waited.

"No. I already told you. The group I was traveling with took everything I had. Can't you just take me as far as the next town? I'm afraid to travel alone."

The older man laughed, an ugly, mean sound. A shiver ran down Sydney's back and she almost turned away. She was still raw from her encounter with Cal and Barrett. She did not want to face any more bad men.

"Do we look like charity do-gooders to you, missy? Besides, you're big enough to take care of yourself. You probably scare off everyone anyway. We'll spend the night here, see if there's anything worth grabbing from the house, but we're leaving without you in the morning."

"You can't leave me. I'm hungry."

Whining again. Sydney willed the woman to shut up. She heard the sound of breaking glass and a door slammed open. The men's voices faded as they entered the farm house. Sydney took advantage of their absence and darted across the back yard to the back wall of the house. She saw a large dark shape sitting on the back steps of the house. She moved closer, until she stood a few feet from the woman.

"Hey." She kept her voice to a soft whisper.

The shape jumped up. "Who's there? Rob! Simon! There's someone here!"

Sydney heard the men curse and she turned to go, but the woman lunged to her feet and threw herself on top of Sydney.

Sydney rolled and tried to squirm out from beneath the woman. "What are you doing? I'm trying to help you!" She needed to get free of this idiot woman. Anger filled her. She kicked her legs to no avail. The woman weighed as much as a small pony.

"Yeah, like I believe you," the woman said. "Then why did you sneak up on me?"

"Because I don't want those two animals in the house to know I'm here. Get off me."

The woman didn't budge. Rob and Simon came out of the house and Sydney knew she was in trouble. A cold finger of fear shivered down her spine.

"Good work, Anna, he coulda killed us in our sleep," said the older man. The other man patted Sydney's body down, looking for weapons.

"Nothing. It's another girl, not a boy." He stood silent for a minute. "I think the two of them could be worth something, Simon. We could sell the big one as a laborer, and depending on how this other one looks in the daylight, we might be able to unload her on Pharaoh."

Sydney could hardly breath, her panic was so great. This was her reward for trying to help a stranger. She couldn't expect any help from Jordan and she prayed that he was smart enough to remain hidden in the barn.

She never should have taken him from his house. If these men took her away how would Jordan make it to a town without her guidance?

"Girly, you got any food?" The one who had patted her down poked her in the side with his foot.

"No." Tears flooded her eyes and she blinked them away. She would not show weakness. Somehow she would find a way to escape and make her way back to Jordan.

"Might as well get some shuteye," said the older man. "I saw a bathroom just inside the back door, we'll shut them in there and take turns watching that they don't escape. Get up, Anna."

He grabbed Anna by the arm and yanked. She yelped but got off Sydney, and none too soon, as Sydney's legs were starting to go numb. Simon grabbed Sydney by the wrist and dragged her into the house. Both women were shoved inside the bathroom and the door slammed shut.

Sydney heard them drag a chair across the floor and she guessed that they had jammed it under the doorknob. The two women were effectively locked inside the tiny room.

"Get out of my way." Sydney tried to push past the large woman, only to realize that there was no room for her companion to step aside. The woman stood crammed up against the toilet in the corner of the bathroom.

"If you can't move at least feel around that wall and see if there's a window." Frustration and anger made Sydney curt with the woman.

"Why do you care if there's a window? It doesn't smell too bad in here."

Sydney sighed. "Because, you idiot, if there's a window,

there's a chance we can escape." She heard the woman run her hand over the wall.

"There's a little one way up high, too small for a person, even a normal-sized one. Don't call me an idiot."

"My apologies. I tend to get a little snippy when I'm being held prisoner in a tiny bathroom with the woman who got me captured when all I wanted to do was save her from some bad men."

Sydney sat on the floor with her back against the door. She needed a plan, and she was worried the men would find Jordan.

She heard the toilet creak as Anna sat down on it. She could sense the woman's bulk in the dark. She was immense, taller than any man Sydney had ever met, and she smelled of old, sour sweat.

"Why did you attack me? I was only trying to help you, you didn't have to sit on me. Now look at the mess we're in."

"You don't have to yell at me. I didn't do anything wrong. I thought you were going to attack me."

Sydney heard the defensiveness in the woman's voice and decided to try a different tactic.

"Where are you from? Your name is Anna, isn't it?" She made her own voice friendly and soft, even though she wanted to throttle the woman for her stupidity.

"Yes. Anna Fielding, what's yours?"

"I'm Sydney, Sydney Waters."

Anna was silent for a moment. "Sidney is a boy's name. Are you a boy?"

"No, I am not a boy, Anna. My name is spelled with a 'y' not an 'i'—that's the female version of Sidney." It was fast becoming obvious that Anna was not the brightest of people. Pops would say she wasn't the sharpest pencil in the box.

"I lived in Decorah," said Anna. "My Daddy ran a feed store just outside of town. He and Mummy were old. They died two months ago of the fever. I tried to keep the store but no one brought me any feed to sell. One day I saw a group of people walking through town and I joined them. Then I met Rob and Simon and they said I could walk with them."

"You do realize that Rob and Simon are bad men, don't you? They're planning to sell you like a slave when you get to a big enough town."

"They wouldn't do that, they're my friends."

"They aren't your—," Sydney clamped her mouth shut and gritted her teeth. She heard the stubborn tone in Anna's voice and knew it would be useless to argue with her. Anna was gullible and believed whatever the two men had told her.

Sydney gave up on conversation. She might as well try to get some sleep; she couldn't do anything until the men let them out of the bathroom.

She wished now she had taken the time to put on her boots. Her feet were getting cold and if she couldn't escape she would be forced to walk barefoot on the gravel road. Her feet would grow raw in no time, crippling her.

She curled up on the floor, used one arm as a pillow, and fell into a fretful sleep.

"Okay, ladies, time to hit the road." The bathroom door flew open and slammed against the outer wall.

Sydney jumped to her feet and groaned. Her body was stiff and sore from being contorted into the small floor space. She rolled her shoulders and neck, trying to work out some of the kinks in her muscles. She looked behind her and her eyes popped wide when she saw her companion in the morning light.

She estimated Anna's height at well over six feet. The woman towered over Sydney's five feet five inches. The wiry black hair that haloed Anna's skull like a bottle brush added several more inches. Her face was very plain and almost too small for her body, with a small, pointed nose and chin and thin lips. Her eyes were her best feature: wide spaced and a beautiful shade of turquoise blue with dark lashes.

Anna shuffled out of the bathroom after Sydney and they exited the house together.

"Looks like we hit the jackpot, Rob," said Simon when they stood before him. "This little girl will fetch us a good price. Look at that pretty face and those green eyes. Beautiful and ex-o-tic, that's what she is. Any whore house will be happy to pay us for her if Pharaoh don't take her."

Sydney narrowed her eyes at the older man. "I'm not your possession to sell. You have no right to hold me prisoner."

Both men laughed. "Sassy, huh? Well, I hate to bust your balloon, missy, but the happy truth is, you are our prisoner, and we can do whatever we want with you. And since we want to sell you, that's what we're gonna do." Simon spat on the ground. "Let's get movin', we're burning daylight. The sooner we get to Driftwood, the sooner we can get paid for you two and get some food."

They tied Sydney's hands in front of her body but left Anna's free. Apparently they felt they had control over the large woman and didn't need to tie her. To Sydney's relief, neither man even glanced at the barn as they escorted Anna and Sydney through the farmyard.

Determined not to show any sign of weakness, Sydney grit her teeth when her bare feet hit the gravel road. She diverted her attention from the pain with thoughts of Jordan.

She hoped that he would be able to hook up with some honest travelers. A blind man wouldn't get very far on his own.

Anna lumbered at her side, humming quietly. Every few minutes she asked Rob and Simon for food, until Simon told her to shut up or they'd leave her right here.

Sydney heard Anna's belly growl and wondered when the group had last eaten. She concentrated on putting one foot in front of the other and willed herself to ignore the small rocks cutting into the soft soles of her feet.

"What's that?"

They had traveled barely a mile up the road. Sydney lifted her head. She felt a strange combination of elation and fear when she saw the trio ahead of them. A man, a dog, and a pony—it had to be Jordan with Dogma and Kria. What was Jordan trying to do?

JORDAN HOPED he had not made a serious miscalculation. When Sid hadn't returned the previous night he had crept to the door of the barn and eavesdropped on the two men long enough to learn that they had taken the boy prisoner. Guilt washed over Jordan. Poor Sid. Captured twice now. The lad wouldn't be in this mess if not for Jordan. Somehow he had to find a way to rescue Sid from the two men.

He owed Sidney. He couldn't admit it to the boy, but he had been terrified of leaving his home. Imagine, a grown man who had traveled the world, afraid to walk down the road. He had depended upon Torrie for so long he hadn't realized how helpless he had allowed himself to become.

Today he had been forced to face his fear of the unknown and he had done okay. Better than okay, in fact. He had even begun to enjoy himself.

Crawling on his hands and knees, Jordan gathered up his things and repacked them. It seemed as if the task took him hours, but by the time he finished he still heard night sounds outside the barn.

He sat on Sidney's sleeping bag to wait for the first

sounds of dawn, afraid that if he laid down he'd fall asleep and miss his opportunity. When he heard a robin chirp he grabbed the walking stick and Kria's lead in one hand, and grabbed Dogma's ruff with the other.

"Road, Dogma. Take us to the road," he whispered. Would she understand? It seemed too much to hope for, but without Dogma's guidance he had no way of knowing which direction to head in.

He hardly dared to breath as they left the shelter of the barn. What if the men were already awake and saw him? He stopped to listen but heard nothing. Now that he was outside he felt a slight warming on his left cheek. Sunrise. Dogma led him south until they hit a gravel road, then stopped.

"Good girl, Dogma. What would I do without you?" He turned to his right, shifting the sun's warmth from his cheek to his back, and headed west. The knowledge that he could tell direction from the heat of the sun cheered him. It was a little thing, but it made him feel less helpless.

He felt certain the men would travel this road as it was close to the farm and headed west. Dogma walked pressed to his hip, guiding him with the pressure of her body. He kept his pace slow and waited for the men and their captives to catch up.

The men stopped a moment and inspected Jordan. "Come on, let's catch up, he might have food," said Rob. "It's only one guy and two of us."

He poked Sydney in the back. "C'mon girl, get a move on." As the men pushed them faster Sydney stumbled and blinked back tears from the pain of her raw feet.

She saw that Jordan was moving very slowly. She thought

of her effort the previous day to experience travel through Jordan's sightless eyes—to walk down an unknown road, unable to see what lay ahead or to either side.

Seeing him in front of her now, without a guide and with no idea of where he was going, she knew that he had to be a very brave man, or a very desperate one, to attempt such a feat. She was beginning to suspect that Jordan was a little of both.

Sydney's group caught up with Jordan in less than five minutes.

He turned around as they approached, his eyes scanning the group. "Good morning." He acted as if he met strangers on the road every day. "How are you all this fine morning?"

Sydney looked at Jordan with surprise and reluctant admiration. She saw no sign of the coddled piano player who had trapped her in his storm cellar. She didn't think the others noticed how tightly Jordan gripped Dogma's fur. It was not obvious that Jordan was a blind man.

"We're in desperate need of food, stranger," said Simon. "Any chance you could help us out?"

Jordan shook his head. "As you can see, I have no supplies," he said.

Smart move, thought Sydney, leaving their things in the barn. She wondered if it was a calculated move, or if it had proven too difficult for him to rig up the bags on Kria's back.

She was amazed that he had haltered the pony without assistance, but then remembered that Torrie had bought Kria for Jordan after the accident. She would've taught her brother how to halter the pony by feel.

They walked together a few minutes in silence. Sydney could feel Rob and Simon's tension increase and she knew they were going to attack Jordan.

"Horse meat is good to eat," said Rob, his tone light. He

left Sydney's side and moved closer to Jordan. "How 'bout if we butcher that plump animal you're leading? He'd feed all of us a few times over."

A look of surprise came over Jordan's face. He faltered a step, then caught himself. "Kria is a prize show animal and a family member. I can't eat her. She'll bring a good price when I get to a town where I can sell her."

The two men flanked Jordan, leaving Sydney and Anna behind. "Maybe you can't eat her, but we can," said Rob. "We're mighty hungry, and the thought of a juicy horse steak is making my mouth water."

Anna stared at Jordan, her brow furrowed. Suddenly it cleared and her eyes lit. Sydney got a sinking feeling in her gut. The giant idiot was going to cause trouble again.

"Hey! I know who you are," said Anna. "You're that famous piano man, Jonas James."

"Jordan James," corrected Jordan. "I'm not sure how famous I am, at least not anymore."

"Jordan, that's right. My parents had all your records. They played your music at the feed store. You can sing too. I know all your songs. I recognized your voice. That's how I know who you are. Hey, aren't you bl-"

Sydney didn't let Anna finish her sentence. She pretended to stumble and pushed her hands into the other woman's body. Anna stumbled, fell forward against Rob, and knocked him down.

Sydney didn't stop to think. She ran forward and drove her hands into Simon's back, knocking him off-balance. "Jordan! Watch out!" She called as Simon grabbed for the back of Jordan's shirt to keep from falling.

"You bitch." Simon recovered and turned toward Sydney. He raised his hand and slapped her hard across the face.

As she fell to her knees she heard a low growl and saw Dogma launch herself at Simon.

Simon screamed when Dogma's massive jaws clamped onto his arm. "Get this dog off me! Rob, get a rock and kill this animal before it destroys my arm."

Rob scrambled to his feet, ran to the side of the road, and picked up a fist-sized rock.

"No sirreebob, you aren't going to hurt any animals," said Anna. She picked up a rock and smashed Rob in the face twice.

Sydney cringed at the sound of Rob's facial bones breaking.

Rob fell to his knees and dropped his rock. He covered his face with his hands. Blood poured out between his fingers.

Sydney looked away, weak-kneed and nauseated.

Anna whirled around and hit Simon in the back of the head. He stumbled forward. She grasped the rock with both hands and brought it down on his head a second time. "Let go of that dog!" She flailed at Simon's head with the rock like a madwoman, her face flushed and twisted with fury. Spittle flew from her lips.

Simon lay on the ground, unmoving, the back of his skull a flattened mass of bloody, matted hair.

"Anna! Anna, stop!" Sydney felt lightheaded. Simon was dead: just like Shannon and Pops, and Cal and Barrett. Was the rest of her life going to be defined by violent death?

Dogma returned to Jordan's side.

Anna stopped in mid-strike. She looked down at Simon's body with a look of satisfaction on her face, tossed down the rock and got to her feet. She wiped her hands on her pants.

"There. He was a bad man," she said.

Sydney looked at the woman and blinked. Apparently

Anna had her own code of what was right and wrong, and Simon had crossed that line. "Uh, Anna, could you please untie me?" She raised up her hands.

"I don't know," said Anna. "I don't think so. Rob and Simon tied you up for a reason."

Sydney looked at Anna in disbelief. "You have got to be kidding me. Anna, Simon and Rob are bad men, you said so yourself. We were their prisoners, remember? They were going to sell us to other bad people. Please untie me."

Her words had no effect. Anna didn't move. She stood and stared at Sydney with her lovely blue eyes.

"Anna, is that your name? Sidney is my friend. Please untie him," said Jordan.

Anna narrowed her eyes. "This Sydney can't be your friend, cause this Sydney is a girl, not a boy."

Sydney couldn't believe this. Anna was worse than an idiot, she was an imbecile. A great big, behemoth nutcase. She looked at Jordan. His face had flushed a deep red.

She recalled the immodest way he had undressed in front of her to bathe and felt her own face flush at the memory. It had been the first time she had seen a naked man and she hadn't torn her eyes away as quickly as she probably should have done.

Actually, she reminded herself, she hadn't torn her eyes away at all. She had been mesmerized by the physical perfection of Jordan's very masculine body: his wide shoulders and well-muscled back, his flat stomach and strong, well-shaped thighs and calves, the patch of golden-brown hair at his groin and what hung below it.

Sydney felt her face grow warm. She gulped and brought her thoughts back to the present.

"Anna, listen to me. Jordan is blind, remember? He only knew my name, and like you, he thought Sydney was a boy's name. He's my friend, honest. I'm his friend. I'm trying to take him someplace safe where we can find people to help him. Please untie me."

Jordan cleared his throat and managed a dry chuckle. "Guess the joke's on me, huh? Anna, we need to go back to the farm for our things. I need your help and I need Sydney's help. Wouldn't you like to be my friend too?"

Anna nodded her head. "Do you have food? I'm hungry."

"Yes, we have food back at the barn," said Sydney. "Now, if we're all friends, could you please untie me. Friends don't keep friends tied up."

Anna hesitated another few moments. Just when Sydney had decided she would never get untied, Anna lumbered over and grabbed her hands. It took her several minutes to work the knots loose with her pudgy fingers.

Once free, Sydney rubbed her wrists for a moment to relieve the chaffing. "Thank you, Anna. Jordan, I'm barefoot and my feet are cut up. I'm going to ride Kria back to the farm while you lead her. Anna can guide us."

Rob lay moaning, half-conscious, where he had fallen in the ditch on the side of the road. Sydney hesitated. Rob was one of the Desperate Ones and couldn't be trusted. If they took him with them he would have to be guarded. Better to leave him to his fate.

She hopped onto Kria's back, grateful that she was pony-sized, and the group returned to the farm. Sydney cleaned her feet and put on her boots. Her feet hurt when she stood, but she would make do. She then served everyone some smoked chicken, boiled up the two eggs the hens had laid for them, and gave the eggs to Anna and Jordan.

Anna sat very close to Jordan, practically pushing him off the straw bale he sat on. Jordan wrinkled his nose and turned his face away with a frown. Sydney bit back a smile. Having spent the night locked in a small room with Anna, she knew how pungent the big woman smelled.

Oblivious to Jordan's reaction, Anna shoveled the food into her mouth and demanded more. Sydney refused. She explained that they had to ration their small supply of meat. She promised to give Anna more food at the midday rest stop. Anna frowned and looked rebellious but Jordan distracted her with questions about her parent's feed store.

While the others talked Sydney repacked the gear on Kria. She discovered the well pump and refilled their water bottles with fresh water. Seeing the pump gave her an idea.

"Anna, it's probably been a while since you were able to have a bath. I found a water pump—would you like to take advantage of the opportunity to clean up before we leave?"

Anna narrowed her eyes at Sydney. "You're going to sneak off while I'm bathing, aren't you?"

Sydney shook her head. "We would never do that. I'll even sit where you can see me while you wash if you like. I just thought, well, you smell a little sweaty. We could rinse out your clothes—it's warm and sunny, so they'll dry fast on your body."

"You're saying I stink." Anna's eyes squinted and her lips scowled.

Sydney looked at the woman. Anna had probably been a magnet for verbal abuse in school. Children had a way of being mean whenever anyone was different, and the big woman was certainly different enough to warrant more than her share of torment. She softened her tone.

"Sorry, I didn't mean to insult you. I get smelly myself when I can't bathe. Everyone does. For me bathing is more of a good health thing. My mother taught me that if we stay clean we get sick less often. It's not easy when we're traveling, so I try to take advantage of every opportunity to wash my body and my clothes. That's okay, you don't have to wash if you don't want to. I was just letting you know that you could."

Anna made small huffing noises and then stood up. "I'd like to clean up," she declared, as if the idea had just occurred to her. "You'll just have to wait for me." She stalked off in the direction of the pump.

Jordan took a deep breath and rubbed his face. "She's not going to be an easy companion, is she?"

Sydney shrugged, then remembered that Jordan couldn't see her gesture. "She seems to like you well enough. I'll just have to be careful how I phrase things around her. Her temper is downright scary and she's a huge woman. You couldn't see her, but she hit Simon like she wanted to beat him to a pulp. Come to think of it, she did beat him to a pulp."

Sydney shuddered. "I never want her mad at me like that."

"That reminds me…," Jordan's voice trailed off. He began again. "I, uh, I'm sorry that I didn't realize you're a girl. It's just, with the name and all, and your voice is pretty husky. I thought you were young, that you hadn't reached puberty so your voice hadn't changed yet. Anyway, I never would have stripped naked in front of you if I had known. That was rude of me. I apologize." His face flushed deep red again.

Sydney grinned. "Don't worry about it. It was an honest mistake. Besides, I didn't look." Yeah, she had, but Jordan didn't need to know that. "When I realized what you were doing I turned around, so your modesty is intact. Let's forget it ever happened."

They sat together in the sun outside the barn in a companionable silence while they waited for Anna to bathe. When she rejoined them her brown polyester pants and flowered blouse were dripping wet but she smelled much less rank.

Sydney had made a decision while waiting for Anna. They were going to head for Driftwood instead of Vermillion. Driftwood was closer than Vermillion by several days travel which would help their limited food supply, especially with an extra large body to feed.

SYDNEY WAS DREAMING AGAIN. Barrett's hollow eye stared at her. Accusing her. Murderess! She had pushed one man to his death in cold blood and bashed in another man's head in anger.

Killer!

Her dead grandfather looked up at her from the cave floor, disapproval written all over his face. She tried to defend her actions but he closed his eyes and refused to listen. She was no better than the men she had killed. She had broken one of the Golden Rules that kept civilization civil: Thou Shalt NOT Kill.

A scrabbling sound penetrated her dream. At first she thought it came from rats, come to feast upon the bodies of Barrett and her grandfather. Her consciousness rose up through the murky depths of her nightmare and she realized the sound came from their packs.

She opened her eyes and turned her head. Anna had the container of smoked chicken open and sat stuffing pieces of it into her mouth.

Sydney leaped to her feet and snatched the container

from Anna's hands. "You fool! What do you think you're doing? This has to feed all of us, and it's not even yours to take."

Sydney was shaking with fury. Feeding a third person was already cutting into their food supply faster than she liked. Despite her rationing efforts she would have to find a new food source within a day or two.

Now Anna was making the problem worse by stealing their food. Sydney checked the container—it was almost empty.

"You stupid, selfish woman. What were you thinking? No, don't tell me; you were hungry." She couldn't disguise her disgust.

Anna narrowed her eyes at Sydney and her expression grew mulish. "I'm bigger than you and you don't feed me enough."

Sydney stared at her in disbelief. Could Anna really be so self-centered? Yes, she could and she was. Over the last few days it had become increasingly apparent that Anna was oblivious to anyone's needs but her own.

Sydney took a deep breath. It wouldn't help matters for her to scold Anna. She would just have to start guarding the food at night.

"Well, you'd better start looking for something else to eat. What's left here belongs to Jordan. And don't even think about the eggs. If you can't behave yourself you'll have to travel on your own—I don't want to travel with someone I can't trust."

She turned away from Anna and placed the chicken container into her pack before collecting the two eggs that the hens laid for them every morning. She boiled them up, peeled them and gave one to Jordan and ate the second one herself.

Anna glowered at Sydney while she ate the egg, her face squinted tight with anger. Sydney ignored her. She didn't care how big and scary Anna was, stealing food from the people who are helping you was just plain wrong.

The single egg didn't make much of a dent in Sydney's empty stomach, but it helped ease some of the hunger pains. She loaded the gear onto Kria and set off down the road without looking to see if Anna was following.

"Something wrong, Syd?" asked Jordan after they had walked several miles without speaking.

In her anger and frustration, Sydney had set a stiff pace. Although Jordan had shown no difficulty keeping up, she eased to a more comfortable walk. It was foolish to punish him for Anna's bad behavior. "Yes," she sighed. "Our Amazonian companion ate most of the food last night while we were sleeping."

Jordan digested the news silently. He knew how hard Sydney had worked to butcher and smoke the chickens and how challenging it was for her to find things to eat on the road. "I'm sorry to hear that. Where is she now?"

"About twenty feet behind us." Sydney kept her voice to a low murmur so Anna wouldn't hear. "She knows I'm angry, not that it matters to her. Anna is downright scary, Jordan. She doesn't seem to possess any sense of right and wrong."

Jordan stroked Dogma's head. "What do you mean, Anna's scary? What am I missing?"

"She's only concerned with what Anna wants, and Anna wants food. Killing Simon yesterday didn't bother her in the least. She's huge, Jordan, almost seven feet tall, and she's massive—not a weak, skinny thing. You should've seen her pick up Rob and toss him into the ditch like he weighed nothing more than a child."

She shuddered as she recalled the way Anna had tossed Rob into the ditch like a piece of useless trash.

Sydney walked in silence for several minutes. Mother Nature was slowly taking back the dirt roads. Thistles, nettles, ragweed, and clovers were creeping into the roadbed from the roadside ditches, breaking up the hard packed earth beneath their feet. She slowed to let Kria snatch tasty bites whenever something attracted her, grateful that she could find food as they traveled.

She sighed. Her life had become too complicated. All she wanted was to find her friend Smokey. How had she ended up caring for a blind piano player and a scary, giant imbecile of a woman? What on earth was she going to do with them?

"I can tell that she's big." Jordan interrupted Sydney's thoughts. "Her voice comes from well over my head and I'm six foot. I can sense her bulk. I don't know what to say about her attitude that would be helpful other than I'm sorry you have to deal with it. I know you have your hands full with me." He turned his warm, gray eyes on Sydney.

She loved the liquid silver of Jordan's eyes. It was a color she had never seen before, part of what made him so attractively unique.

She reached out and gave Jordan's arm a quick pat. "You're easy to deal with, piano man. Fortunately Anna idolizes you. At least we know she'll never hurt you. I'm not so confident when it comes to my safety however. Her brain isn't wired right, and I have to be honest, I think she can be dangerous. Now that she's latched onto us—onto you—I doubt that we can get rid of her, but I'd sure like to see her leave. She makes me more nervous than a spider on a hot fry pan."

When they stopped to camp at the end of the day Sydney pointed out a raspberry patch to Anna and divided the remainder of the chicken jerky between herself and Jordan, giving Jordan the major portion. She joined Anna and picked as many berries as she could find, almost filling the empty chicken container. At least they would have something for breakfast.

She placed her sleeping bag near Jordan, set the chicken cages between them, and tied Kria to a small tree near their heads. She placed the berry container into the foot of her sleeping bag before she crawled into it.

Anna sat on a downed tree twenty feet away and watched Sydney with a scowl on her face.

Sydney could feel the waves of anger pulsing her way. Survival wasn't about winning a popularity contest and she knew that right now she was very unpopular with the large woman. For her own safety she needed to keep an eye on Anna.

It wouldn't surprise Sydney if Anna tried to take a rock to her head while she slept. She spent the night dozing in short naps and awoke at dawn feeling as if she hadn't slept at all.

Anna loomed over her. "I'm hungry. I want breakfast."

Sydney scrambled out of her bag and forced herself to take a leisurely stretch to mask her fear. She pointed to the raspberry patch. "The berry patch is over there. That's your breakfast."

Anna didn't move. "You picked a whole bunch last night. I saw you. Why can't I have those?"

"Because, Anna, I picked those to share with Jordan. If you hadn't eaten most of our jerky I would share that with you too, but now we don't have any food left. You'll have to fend for yourself, just as we do. I have to find food for myself and Jordan. I can't feed you as well."

Jordan woke up during their exchange and folded his blankets. He stopped and faced Anna. "Anna, things are tough out here for you, I know. They're tough on all of us. You have to pull your own weight and part of that means finding food for yourself. We'll help when we can, but you have to learn to depend on yourself, in case we're not around. I know you can do it. You're a strong, healthy woman. Sydney would be happy to point out things that are good to eat, right Sydney?"

Sydney shot Jordan a grateful look, and remembered again that he couldn't see it. Funny how she kept forgetting he was blind. "Jordan's right. I'd be glad to help you when I can, Anna. If you want to go pick berries now I'll boil up one of the eggs for you."

The scowl on Anna's face cleared and she moved off to the berry patch.

Sydney huffed out a heavy sigh. "Thanks, Jordan. I think we need to find more people to join up with, or a place to try to leave her. I do believe that girl would kill me for food."

Jordan shook his head. "I won't let that happen. Dogma usually hunts at night but we'll keep her close for the next few nights. She won't let Anna hurt you."

The rest of the day passed without incident. Jordan and Sydney walked side by side, their pace steady. Once their arms brushed against each other. The contact felt like an electric current and made Sydney's pulse jump. She talked about her father's work, and how he had instilled a reverence for nature in her, to cover up her reaction.

Anna followed a short distance behind, silent and brooding.

Late in the afternoon Sydney spied a hickory grove and decided to stop for the night. She showed Anna how to find the green husks that covered the nuts and roll them off with her foot. She smashed the shells with a rock and picked out the nutmeat. It was slow going but the nuts were sweet and a welcome change from berries.

"Why can't we eat the chickens?" asked Anna. Her big fingers were clumsy and she grew frustrated trying to pick the small bits of hickory meat from the smashed shells.

"Because the hens are more useful right now for their eggs. They provide us with food every day and they fend for themselves. If we kill them and eat them we'll get one meal and then that's it. We'll be hungry again with no eggs. Can you understand that?"

Sydney stopped separating shells from the smashed nuts and looked at Anna. Anna was scowling again, a look Sydney knew meant she was unhappy and frustrated. Sydney sighed inwardly. Keeping Anna happy was a Herculean task.

For a brief moment she wished she had stayed on her grandfather's farm. As lonely as that had been, it was easier than dealing with Jordan and Anna. Although, she reminded herself, Jordan had turned out to be much easier to care for than she had anticipated. He did everything for himself that he could, and grew more capable every day.

"Here, let's work together on these," she said after she watched a frustrated Anna toss away good nutmeat. "You collect the nuts and smash them, and I'll pick out the edible bits. When I've filled my container I'll see if I can scare up a squirrel or two for dinner. Sound fair?"

Anna agreed and they spent the next two hours processing hickory nuts. Sydney processed a few extra and gave them to Anna to keep her quiet while she hunted. She had noticed several squirrels scampering in the hickory trees and hopping across the ground with nuts in their mouths. She was confident she could bag a couple with a little effort.

Sydney pulled two arrows for her crossbow pistol and

noted that she had only two left. She would need to make time to replenish her ammunition soon.

Forty minutes later she had two squirrels butchered and turning on a spit over a small fire. She gave one to Anna and split the second one with Jordan.

Despite her hunger, Sydney could only manage a few bites of the squirrel meat. The last time she had prepared squirrel was the day she had murdered Cal and Barrett. The memory of that day twisted her gut and robbed her of her appetite. She gave the remainder of her portion to Jordan and told him she had gorged on nuts.

Jordan took the squirrel and wished Sydney would talk to him about whatever torment ate at her. He knew she had to be as hungry as he was. Why couldn't she eat? During the days he tried to find a way to politely pry while they walked, but Sydney was adept at turning away his probing questions.

He knew something terrible had happened to Sydney—her nightmares were proof of it. She thought he didn't know about her bad dreams, but Jordan was a light sleeper and he heard her thrashing and moaning in her bag.

Sydney's fear of the Desperate Ones led him to believe that they were at the heart of her trouble, but whenever he brought them up she changed the subject.

Jordan set down the piece of squirrel, careful to keep his hand on the plate so Anna wouldn't steal it. He wished Sydney trusted him more.

He had made a terrible mistake imprisoning her in the storm cellar. He should have simply told her the truth and asked for her help. Of course, then he had believed Syd was a boy.

He had been shocked when Anna told him Sydney was a girl. Christ, he had stripped bare in front of her. Even now he felt his face flush at the memory. Any other girl would think he was some sort of rude lout, but Sydney had laughed her wonderful, husky laugh and told him not to worry about it. He could tell she meant it.

One thing he had learned about his companion, there wasn't an insincere bone in Sydney's body.

He had changed since she had taken him from his family home. Now he could admit to himself that he had been terrified to leave everything familiar and strike out into the unknown.

Yet here he was. Every day he gained a little more confidence in his ability to deal with a strange and unknown world. He felt safe walking between Dogma and Sydney.

He had changed in more practical ways as well. His ability to detect objects kept growing stronger.

Jordan let his sightless gaze roam over their night camp. He picked out Anna, sitting on the ground across the fire. He heard her smack her lips as she ate.

He looked for Kria and found her tethered to his right. He turned his head to look behind him and found Sydney lying in her bag next to the chicken cages.

He couldn't see her of course, but he sensed her what—aura? Energy? The best way he could describe it was to say that he felt things.

Sydney's shallow, ragged breathing told him she was awake and still troubled. He gave Dogma the remainder of Sydney's squirrel and felt for the washing pot Sydney had placed near him.

Even as a young boy he hated to be dirty. He could hear Torrie tease him about his almost pathological need to be clean. "You're so fastidious, Jordan!"

His breath caught for a moment. He missed his sister almost more than he could bear. Torrie had been everything to him: mother, father, sister, friend, critic, business manager. He had relied on her for everything and she had never let him down.

He stopped washing as a new thought struck him. Perhaps he had relied on his sister for too much. Without her to care for him he was forced to stretch himself, to become more than just a blind piano player who also sang. It was time for him to grow up and become a man.

A slow, satisfied smile crept over Jordan's face.

"So, do you have a plan?" asked Jordan the next morning.

Six days had passed since Anna killed Simon. Sydney had pushed a steady, but not taxing, walking pace. Her fears of traveling with Jordan had disappeared as he readily adapted to life on the road. His uncanny sense of radar seemed to have strengthened and her constant worry about him had eased.

Altho Dogma left them for brief hunting forays during the day now, he rarely stumbled. A pothole could surprise him now and then, but she discovered that if she called out the depression—"hole, one o'clock, five feet ahead"—he was usually able to avoid it.

Anna still posed an annoying problem. Sydney managed her as best she could during the day while Dogma continued to guard Sydney at night. She wished they could find someplace to leave the woman. Traveling with an unpredictable killer was stressful and took much of the pleasure out of the trip.

Did she have a plan? Sydney debated how to answer Jordan's question. She needed to find a new home for her companions before she continued with her quest to find Smokey. Once they came to a town, a big, strong woman like Anna should be able to find work in exchange for food and a bed.

Jordan was a whole different problem. She couldn't just leave him with anyone. She liked Jordan and needed to find someone trustworthy and kind to look after him. She wished she knew how to go about that task.

"Anna can work for her keep, but I might be more difficult to place," Jordan continued. "I don't want you to worry. I can sing for my supper you know. Literally."

Sydney cleared her throat. "To be honest I've been a little worried about that. I can't decide if we're better off heading into one of the towns, or if we should try to find a farm that's still functioning. What do you think?"

"A town, definitely. A town will have a bar or tavern where I can play and more opportunities for Anna."

"Rob and Simon were headed to Driftwood, South Dakota. I thought we might check it out. According to my maps it's about two more days travel from here."

Jordan turned his face toward her and smiled.

Since they had left his home he had stopped shaving and his beard had taken hold. Sydney noticed that it gleamed with red-gold highlights in the sun's rays. His hair had lightened as well.

Her heart skipped a beat. Jordan James was a handsome man, there was no denying that. No wonder women loved him. She hadn't heard him sing, but judging from the number of trophies he had won he must be very good.

"Driftwood it is then," he said. "I'm sure we'll work it all out when we get there."

They walked several miles in silence. Jordan surprised Sydney by reaching out and feeling for her hand. He laced his fingers through hers. "My sister used to walk with me like this. I miss the human contact. Do you mind?"

Sydney shook her head, remembered he couldn't see her, and squeezed his fingers. "Not at all. I miss human contact too." Her voice rasped with sudden tears.

"You haven't told me much about yourself, Sydney. Where are you from and why are you traveling?" Jordan expected Sydney to deflect his questions, but she surprised him and answered.

"I grew up on my grandfather's farm near the Mississippi River in Iowa," Sydney replied. "My dad worked for the Fish and Wildlife Service as a biologist and an educator. He traveled a lot. Mom and my sister Shannon and I lived with Pops, my mom's father, on his sheep farm, and Dad joined us whenever he could.

"My mother was an artist, a painter. Dad was in Yellowstone Park speaking at a convention when the world went crazy. Mom was opening her latest show in New York. When they hadn't come back to us after a year we knew they both had died."

Sydney's throat tightened. "Then Shannon and Pops were murdered by Desperate Ones and I couldn't bear to stay alone at the farm. I decided to see if I could find my friend Smokey."

Although she kept her tone light, Sydney felt the still raw pain of her family's deaths. She swallowed the lump in her throat, grateful that Jordan couldn't see the tears hanging in her eyes.

"I'm so sorry," he said. "That must have been awful for you. Then you find me and I lock you in a storm cellar. Nice guy, huh? I can't tell you how awful I feel that I did that to you."

He clasped the hand he held between both of his for a moment and then stroked it. "I hope you can forgive me."

The hand stroking felt good, soothing. It reminded Sydney of how her mother used to rub her back when Sydney was upset.

"Don't worry about it. You needed help, and I was focused on my own issues. That was probably the only way you could have gotten me to stay. Now I'm glad I did."

It surprised Sydney to realize that in spite of the issues caused by Jordan's lack of sight, she honestly did feel glad that she had brought him with her. Jordan James had become an excellent and entertaining traveling companion.

Jordan stopped stroking and squeezed her hand. "Still, my selfish need was no excuse for holding you prisoner."

Sydney thought of Cal and Barrett. "We do what we have to do, Jordan. No worries, okay? I mean it. It's forgotten." She looked back to check on Anna, happily munching on some apples Sydney had found earlier.

Jordan said nothing for a bit. "Who is this Smokey guy you're going to find?"

"He's a friend. He worked for my grandfather one summer when Dad couldn't be there to help and Pops was laid up with a bad knee. Smokey is a neat guy. His grandmother is the shaman of his tribe and he taught me some interesting things while he was with us."

"Does he know you're coming?" Jordan hated the stab of jealousy that cut through him when Sydney spoke about her friend Smokey.

"No, how could he? Although, the way Smokey talked about his grandmother I wouldn't be surprised if she knew. It doesn't matter—I have nowhere else to go. I only hope he'll be at his grandmother's. Why do you ask?"

Jordan lifted one shoulder. "Just curious. I was hoping

that when I found a place to live that you might stay with me for a while, help me get settled in. It would be good to have a friend around and we seem to get along all right–"

Sydney cut into his words. "We'll cross that bridge when we get to it. I need to find my friend."

What she didn't say aloud was that she needed to find Smokey to help her deal with her role in Shannon's death and her growing lack of remorse over killing Barrett and Cal. She needed Smokey's help to get back on the right path.

Sydney kept them zig-zagging west and north until she was on the same latitude as Driftwood, then headed straight west. The countryside underwent a radical change. Eons of windblown sediment carried from the plains had collected and compressed into hills known as the Loess Hills.

The change in scenery cheered Sydney. One state nearly down. One and a half more to go—straight across South Dakota to Wyoming.

She checked the next map and calculated the distance to their destination. "We should be able to see Driftwood by this time tomorrow," she announced. "We'll have to decide how we want to approach it. Any ideas?"

"Will they have food?" asked Anna.

"Yes, Anna, I'm sure they'll have food. You'll have to work for it—you do realize that, don't you?"

Anna stared blankly at Sydney.

Did Anna understand the concept of working for a living? Did her parents teach her to be responsible for herself? Not my problem, Sydney decided. Anna would have to learn to care for herself. "Any useful ideas? Jordan?"

"I think we should try to find an outlying farm where we can get information and find out what's going on in Drift-wood, who's in charge, if anybody, before we enter the town. We don't want to walk in blindly—so to speak." He grinned.

Sydney nodded in agreement and then voiced it aloud. She wondered how long it would take her to remember that Jordan couldn't see her. She pushed them farther and longer that afternoon to ensure they would hit Driftwood on the morrow.

The next morning brought storm clouds brewing low on the western horizon. She got everyone on the road early, hoping they could find shelter before the storm found them. Her little tarp was only big enough to provide cover for one person and she suspected Anna would be unhappy left sitting out in the rain.

She kept the group moving at a lively clip, and by midday they could see the town of Driftwood sprawled out on the prairie next to the sparkling Missouri River. Eager to reach their destination, Sydney refused to stop for lunch and handed out the last of the apples to eat while they walked.

By mid-afternoon they came abreast of a well-kept farm just as the dark storm clouds closed overhead and scattered drops of rain began to fall. The wind picked up and whipped their clothing around their bodies. The chickens squawked with displeasure as their cages bounced against Sydney's pack.

Sydney could see the dark curtain of heavy rain falling over Driftwood and quickened her steps. The temperature dropped several degrees and she knew the rainstorm was about to reach them. They needed to find shelter fast.

With the others pressed close around her, Sydney turned down the farm's drive and headed for the nearest shed. Long and low, it was a single-story wooden structure with a large sliding door at one end and no windows. She heaved her weight against the door and got it open wide enough for Kria to squeeze through with his packs. She herded everyone inside, and shut the door against the wind.

She stood for a minute to let her eyes adjust to the gloomy light. The shed held only a large black SUV with "Lady Doc" vanity license plates.

"Whew! I wasn't sure we'd make shelter before that storm hit. I was afraid we were going to get hit with hail."

No sooner were the words out of Sydney's mouth when they heard the clatter of hail on the shed's tin roof. The noise was deafening. She shouted at Anna and Jordan to get inside the vehicle, commanded Dogma to hop in the rear, and then quickly took the packs and lead rope off Kria before she crawled into the driver's seat.

Kria darted about the shed for a minute and then settled down in a corner where a patch of grass had grown up inside the shed.

The vehicle helped to muffle the sound of the pounding hail. The seats, covered in buttery soft leather, were deep and comfortable. Jordan lowered the back of the passenger seat, sighed, and went to sleep. Anna laid down on the rear seat and began to snore.

Sydney tried to stay alert, but fatigue overtook her. She lowered her seat back and promptly fell asleep with the others.

"Sydney? Syd." Jordan's breath was soft in her ear. She turned her face toward his, unable to see anything in the dark.

"What?" she whispered back, half asleep. His mouth was only inches from hers. The urge to cross those few inches and touch his lips with her own jolted her awake. Shaken, she fumbled for the seat control and raised the seat back to remove the temptation.

"I feel someone moving in the shed."

Sydney opened her eyes wide and tried to catch movement outside the SUV, but could see nothing in the dark. It was possible that Jordan was mistaken, but she trusted his radar-sense. He was rarely wrong.

She sat and waited in the same way she would in the forest if she was Slow Walking. Finally she detected a small motion in the dark. She let out her breath.

"Ha, it's just Kria moving around," she said with relief. She felt Jordan shake his head.

"No. There are two bodies moving—one is Kria, the other is a person. I'm sure of it. I can sense her."

"Her?"

"It feels like a woman."

Sydney strained her eyes, tried to feel what Jordan felt. Anna snored in the back seat, covering any sound from outside the vehicle. Dogma was in the far back cargo hold, silent but alert. Sydney wondered why she wasn't growling. Apparently Jordan was thinking the same thing.

"I wonder what's wrong with Dogma. She should have noticed whoever it is by now and warned us," he said.

SYDNEY POPPED OPEN HER DOOR. "Who's out there?" she demanded as she climbed out of the driver's seat. She heard a rustle of cloth and soft footsteps approached her.

"Melody Hebrig. This is my farm. Who are you?"

The woman's voice sounded mature, sure of herself. Sydney guessed her age to be in the mid-thirties. She heard no fear in Melody's voice, and more important, no menace.

"I'm a traveler, Sydney Waters. I have two companions in the car, plus a seeing eye dog and our pony, Kria, is in the shed."

"Ah, yes, it was Kria who called me out here."

Melody's words confused Sydney—she had not heard Kria calling or making any noise in the shed.

"I don't understand. We were all very quiet, we couldn't have disturbed you. We were only seeking shelter from the storm," said Sydney.

"You were quiet. Kria is thirsty and I heard her asking for water. Animals don't have to talk aloud for me to understand them. Do you have a lead for your pony? If not I'm sure she'll follow me to the barn. I can bed her down and give her feed and water there."

Kria nickered at the woman's words.

Sydney smiled. "Sounds as if she understood you. There's a lead around here somewhere. I think I hung it off your car's side mirror—yes, here it is." She slid the lead off the mirror and held it out.

Melody groped for it and then took it from Sydney and slid it onto Kria. Sydney marveled at how easily she haltered the pony in the darkness.

"Why don't you get your friends and come with me?" Melody said. "I have food up at the house and something to feed your dog as well." She pushed the shed door open wider and led Kria out into the night.

"I heard all that," said Jordan as he crawled out of the passenger side. "Should we leave sleeping beauty in the back seat until she awakens? Please?"

"Good idea. I'm sure she'll find us in the morning. Let me get Dogma and grab the chickens." Sydney quietly let Dogma out the rear door and then balanced the chicken cages over one shoulder. She led the way out of the shed with Dogma and Jordan close on her heels.

Melody and Kria were just disappearing around the corner of a barn to her right. Sydney grabbed Jordan's hand and grasped the chicken cages so they wouldn't fall off her shoulder. She quickened her steps to catch up with the other woman.

Once inside the large barn Sydney set the chickens down. They squawked and then settled back to sleep. She could see by Melody's lantern that they were standing in the central aisle of a horse barn. Disturbed by the newcomers, animals moved quietly in stalls on both sides of the aisle.

She heard Melody talking to Kria in a stall to her left. She approached the woman and waited outside the stall as Melody placed straw bedding, then hay on the floor for Kria.

"There's water in the hanging bucket," said Melody. "I always keep an extra stall or two prepared just in case. I never know when someone's going to show up with an injured animal."

She took Kria's lead off, exited the stall, and hung the lead on a hook. "She'll be much happier here with food and water and companions. Follow me, please. I'll make us some hot chicory and breakfast. It's a little early but if you've been traveling I'm sure you could use some food." She led the way out of the barn toward the house.

The faint gray light of predawn showed a small, two-story house with a central chimney rising up above the roof peak. Melody led them to the left side of the house and into a mudroom. "Boots off here, please. I try to keep the house as clean as I can." She slipped off her own muck boots and padded into the kitchen.

Sydney followed suit and led Jordan by the hand into the kitchen. A large round table sat in the center of the room. She pulled out a wooden chair from the table and placed Jordan's hand on the chair. "You can sit here." She took a seat next to him and looked around her.

A kerosene camp lantern sat in the center of the table and lit the large room with a soft, yellow light. Braided rugs covered the floor under the table and in front of the sink. Blue and white cafe curtains hung at a row of paned windows, their sills filled with plants. A rocking chair sat next to a wood stove on the interior wall behind her.

The homey normality of the room brought a lump to Sydney's throat. "How do you find fuel? My family ran out a year ago," she asked, surprised to see the working lantern.

Melody lit the gas stove and moved a large pot of something over the burner before she answered. "I'm the local doctor. I'm a veterinarian, but after the real doc died I was pressed into service." Her voice held a bitter note. "The man who runs Driftwood keeps me supplied in case I have to work at night." Melody moved around the kitchen gathering plates and cups.

Sydney watched her work, impressed with her smooth efficiency. Melody was taller than Sydney, long-legged and built boyishly lean. Her blonde hair was cut short, framing a square face with wide-spaced blue eyes and a straight, thin nose.

The heady aroma of ground chicory root filled the room and several minutes later she placed steaming clay mugs in front of Sydney and Jordan. Melody took a swallow from her own cup and checked the pot of food before she joined them at the table.

"So, tell me your story. How did you end up in my shed?"

Sydney gave a brief account of their travels while Jordan sat silently sipping his chicory.

Melody turned her attention to him. "I know who you are of course, you were quite the phenomenon. It is rather brave of you to journey into the unknown when you can't see."

Jordan shrugged. "I had no choice. When I lost my sister I knew it would be impossible for me to survive on my own. I'm fortunate that Sydney came along when she did. She's good and kind and has a generous soul."

Sydney stared down at her cup and inwardly squirmed at Jordan's words. She should confess that she wasn't good, she was evil, an unrepentant murderess, but she couldn't say the words. She wanted Jordan to think well of her.

"Can you tell us about Driftwood?" she asked the doctor.

Melody's face hardened. She stood up and went to the stove and checked the now bubbling pot. Satisfied with the temperature of the stew, Melody served up three large bowls.

The food smelled wonderful and Sydney's stomach growled with hunger. They ate in silence other than an occasional groan of pleasure from both Sydney and Jordan. The stew was not only hot, it was full of meat and vegetables and herbs. Sydney couldn't help herself—when her bowl was empty she picked it up and licked it clean.

Melody smiled at her. "Well, that makes the cook feel good," she said. "I'm glad you liked it." She cleared away their dishes and refilled their mugs before sitting down.

"Why do you want to go to Driftwood?" she asked. "If I were you I'd wait until nightfall and sneak around the town. Get as far away as you can. There's too much trouble there."

"What do you mean, trouble? What kind of trouble?" asked Sydney. "We're looking for a place where Jordan will be looked after and maybe provide an opportunity for him to continue with his music in return for room and board. We also need a place for our other companion. We left her sleeping in your car."

Sydney frowned, searching for the right words to describe Anna. "We met up with Anna a couple weeks ago. She's not the easiest or most pleasant person to deal with. She has a temper and a rather limited focus. I'm not quite sure what to think of her. She scares the crap out of me, to be honest."

Melody's eyes narrowed and she frowned. "In what way does she scare you Sydney?"

"Well, she's big—very, very big—and she has a temper and she also seems to be missing the gene that tells her what's right and what's wrong. All she cares about is food, which under the circumstances isn't that surprising I guess. I get the feeling she would kill me for something to eat and feel no

remorse. She does seem to like animals. That's the only positive thing I can say about Anna."

"If she likes animals she'll like it here. I have plenty to eat."

"What did you mean about trouble in Driftwood, Miss
Melody?" asked Jordan. He had pushed his chair away from
the table and sat with his long legs extended in front of him,
ankles crossed. He slouched against the back of the chair
with his arms crossed over his chest and relaxed.

Sydney glanced sideways at Jordan. Despite his leanness,
it was hard not to notice the way his tee stretched across his
chest and arm muscles. He looked strong and masculine
sitting in Melody's feminine kitchen.

Jordan's maleness gave her an unexpected warm feeling
in her abdomen. She forced her attention back to Melody.

"Driftwood sits twenty miles east of Penton. Penton had
three jails: a federal penitentiary, a minimum security jail for
juvenile offenders, and the town jail for the regular
scofflaws."

Sydney's stomach clenched. She thought of the Desperate
Ones and wasn't sure she wanted to hear Melody's story.

Melody moved to the rocking chair by the wood stove.
"When The Upheaval happened the prison systems broke
down and the criminals were released. No one wanted to be
responsible for the inmates starving to death in their cells, so
the men in charge set them free."

"How many inmates were turned loose on the town?"
asked Jordan.

"Hundreds. As you can imagine, it went bad fast. Because
Penton relied on the jail and prison for jobs, they didn't have
the farming infrastructure to provide food for their citizens.
That's where Driftwood came in. We grew the food, raised
meat and dairy, and provided other goods and services to
Penton. It didn't take the criminals long to figure out that

they would starve to death in Penton and they made their way here."

"What happened when they got here? Were you ready for them?" asked Jordan. "I'm sure there are many stupid people in prison, but there are smart ones too. They wouldn't kill the people who make their food."

"Unfortunately many innocent people died while the prison gangs fought out their new hierarchy in the town. Eventually one gang took over Driftwood, and their leader, a megalomaniac who goes by the name of 'Pharaoh', is currently our self-appointed mayor."

Sydney had a sick feeling in her stomach. The two men who had been traveling with Anna had mentioned selling her and Anna to Pharaoh. Driftwood did not sound like the kind of place that would welcome and care for a blind musician.

Melody took a deep, shuddering breath. "To control those who live in the surrounding area and provide food, Pharaoh took hostages. Someone from every family. Young children and women mostly. He left the able-bodied men to work the farms. We're forced to comply to keep our loved ones safe."

Sydney looked at Melody in horror. "I can't believe they're holding women and children hostage. That's-that's sick. Why don't the farmers fight Pharaoh?" Outrage at the wrongness of the situation filled her. Bile rose in her throat. She couldn't drink any more tea and she set the mug down.

Melody's hand trembled. "You don't understand. We have no choice. We do what we have to do. The hostages are kept under guard in an old dairy barn. They're starving and living in their own filth. A few have died. When that happens Pharaoh sends out his men to grab another hostage."

Melody looked at Sydney, her eyes filled with pain. "He has my husband. When the town's doctor was killed they came and took Alan. Pharaoh's gang likes to fight and they need a doctor fairly often. It doesn't matter that I'm a veterinarian, they figure I can patch them up well enough. They know I wouldn't take care of their wounds unless they had something powerful to hold over me."

Her tone became bitter. "The only blessing is that Alan and I didn't have any children for Pharaoh to take. Most of the others weren't so lucky. Pharaoh prefers to take the kids hostage because they can't fight back and they need less food to survive."

Suddenly the warm friendly kitchen felt cold and less safe. "You're right," said Sydney. "I don't understand. How can a person do that to another human being? Why do you let them? Why don't you band together and rescue your loved ones?"

Melody shook her head. "We tried once. They killed several kids to teach us a lesson, then grabbed more to replace them. We can't thwart Pharaoh by leaving the area because we have loved ones locked up who need us. If we try to leave, Pharaoh will kill them. So we stay, and sneak extra food in to them when we can. As long as he has the children he's essentially holding the entire community of Driftwood hostage."

The trio sat in silence for several minutes. Rays of sunlight streamed through the window as the sun broke the horizon. The normalcy of the sunshine felt wrong to Sydney after hearing Melody's story.

She reached down and scratched the back of Dogma's head. She felt so tired. The strain of looking after another person and keeping an eye on Anna had worn her out. Her eyes closed and her chin dropped. She'd decide what to do about Jordan tomorrow.

20

SYDNEY OPENED her eyes and gazed around her. She was lying in a twin bed, warm and cozy with fresh sheets and a quilt wrapped around her. Sunlight blazed through the window at her side. She rolled away from it, punched the pillow under her head to a more comfortable position and snuggled into the bedclothes.

Her eyes popped open a moment later. Was this a dream? Were Shannon and her grandfather down in the kitchen waiting for her? A bubble of excitement welled briefly in her chest, then slowly deflated as she took a closer look at the room. A low pine chest sat under the window and unfamiliar artwork hung on the wall.

She was in Melody Hebrig's house. She recalled the vet urging her up the stairs and into the bed after she had fallen asleep at the table. The weight of her situation came crashing in on her. Driftwood sounded like a nightmare—not a safe place to leave a blind piano player.

Sydney crawled out of the warm bed and immediately missed its safety and comfort. She turned to crawl back under the quilt but stopped. Much as she'd like to, she couldn't hide from her life, couldn't undo what had been done. There were decisions for her to make and actions for her to take.

She looked around for her clothes and found them missing. A set of Melody's clothing sat in their place. She put them on, grateful for something clean to wear. Melody's legs were longer than Sydney's and the jeans fit snug on her rounder bottom. She rolled the cuffs to take up the extra leg length and padded barefoot out of the bedroom into a wide hallway.

Daylight streamed in windows on either end of the hall. Two rooms stood opposite hers, a fourth beside it. She stuck her head into the room directly opposite and watched Jordan sleep. He snored lightly, little phut, phut noises that escaped his slightly parted lips.

Dogma lay curled on a rug beside Jordan's bed, head on her paws. She thumped her tail when she saw Sydney in the doorway. Sydney smiled at the greeting and spoke softly to the dog before she turned and made her way to the staircase.

She looked briefly into the bedroom next to hers. Also on the east side of the house, sunlight streamed into the pleasant space through a large bay window. Red and blue braided rugs were scattered around a queen-size, Shaker style bed. An intricate blue and white star quilt covered the bed's surface with more quilts folded and piled on a chair in the corner.

This had to be Melody's room. It looked warm and inviting and lived in.

She saw a large, framed photo on the dresser and slipped inside the room to get a closer look. She picked up the photo and took it to the window to study it. In it, a younger, smiling Melody stood with a handsome, dark haired man. The man had an arm wrapped possessively around Melody's shoulder, hugging her close to his side. His face beamed with love and pride.

This must be Melody's husband Alan, decided Sydney. She felt a sharp stab of pain. The picture reminded Sydney of the love her parents had once shared. She set the photo back where she'd found it and left the bedroom to finish her exploring.

Expecting a fourth bedroom, Sydney was surprised to find a well-used office or study in the remaining room. The four walls were lined with floor-to-ceiling shelves that overflowed with books stacked every which way. A large oak desk sat in the center of the room with a microscope, slides, and papers scattered across its surface. A brown leather chair, its surface cracked with age and use, sat next to the desk.

Sydney itched to check out the books, to sit and read in the welcoming space, but she recognized the room as private space.

She headed down the stairs but stopped halfway when she heard Anna in the kitchen below talking to Melody. Sydney sank down on a step and eavesdropped. She knew it was wrong to listen like this, but she felt no desire to see Anna. She wished the woman would go somewhere else so Sydney wouldn't ever have to deal with her again.

The force of her dislike for Anna surprised Sydney and made her feel a little guilty. Anna couldn't help who she was.

No, that wasn't true, thought Sydney. Everyone can try to be a better person. Anna didn't make any effort. She expected everyone to do for her and that's what Sydney disliked most about her.

"I'm still hungry."

Sydney sighed. How could Anna be so rude? She should be grateful that Melody was feeding her.

"Sorry, Anna, but you've finished your share of the oatmeal. I have to save the rest for Sydney and Jordan." Melody's tone was mild yet firm.

"Why? Sydney ate my food. She made me go hungry. She wouldn't share. I don't like to be hungry."

"I find that hard to believe, Anna. Sydney seems like a fair and generous person. Why would she withhold food from you?"

"I dunno. She did, I swear. She was mean to me. She made me pick berries and nuts. I want more oatmeal."

"I'm sorry, Anna, but you need to share or else leave my kitchen. You've already eaten an extra portion of oatmeal. I don't believe you're as hungry as you say you are. You just think you're hungry. It's time for you to think of things other than food."

Sydney grimaced. It wasn't right for her to stick Melody with Anna. She stood and descended the remaining stairs. "Good mornin', Melody, Anna." She forced a cheerful note into Anna's name when she saw the woman's scowling face.

"There you are, Sydney, good morning. You look a little more rested. I trust you slept well? Do my clothes fit okay?"

Sydney sat at the table, her attention on Anna. "Yes to all those questions, Melody. Thank you for everything. You've been very kind. I said good morning, Anna. How are you this morning?"

Anna's scowl deepened. "I'm still hungry and Melody won't feed me."

"From what I heard you've had your breakfast, Anna. Perhaps you should thank Melody for sharing what she has with you, and try not to be so demanding."

Melody set a bowl of steaming oatmeal in front of Sydney.

Anna's eyes riveted on the bowl and she smacked her lips.

"Thank you Melody, it's a real treat to have a hot breakfast," said Sydney. "You know Anna, I think I may have a solution to your hunger problem. What would you think about working in a kitchen? You could wash dishes and pots and pans in exchange for your meals. That way you'd get fed three meals every day and maybe snacks in between. How does that sound?"

Anna's face brightened and she nodded. "This kitchen?"

Sydney shook her head. She ate some of the oatmeal before she answered, savoring the honey-sweetened porridge studded with dried apple bits. "No, not here. It would have to be a restaurant-sized kitchen. I thought we could go into Driftwood today and look for a place that needs help. What do you think, Melody?"

Melody frowned. "Sydney, I don't mind you leaving Jordan and Dogma here at all, but I'm not so sure it's a good idea for you to go into Driftwood on your own. Attractive young women have a way of disappearing inside Pharaoh's private harem and are rarely seen again."

"What's a harem?" asked Anna. She was watching Sydney eat with the focus of a hungry dog waiting to see if the smallest scrap of food will be tossed to her.

"It's a place where women are forced to have sex with any man who wants her," replied Melody. Her voice was tight with anger. "Pharaoh's men have kidnapped young women—some were wives, some were daughters too young for sex—and pressed them into service for himself and his court of followers. Honestly, Sydney, I think you would be wise to rest here for a of couple days and then forget Driftwood. Be smart and head to the next town. Bad things happen to attractive young women here."

"What about Anna? Can I leave her here?" Sydney didn't want to take Anna on the road with her again. She'd rather face Pharaoh then have to spend one more day wondering if Anna was going to attack her for food.

"Most jobs are taken, especially ones connected with food, but I could ask around for you."

Sydney pushed the remainder of her oatmeal away, her stomach suddenly tied up in knots. Anna grabbed the bowl and greedily finished it.

Sydney watched Anna with a faint feeling of disgust. "Isn't there anything that can be done about Pharaoh? Can't you get lawmen to come from another town to take care of these guys?"

Melody shook her head and joined them at the table. "No one dares to mess with Pharaoh and his men. I told you last night that the sanctity of life has no meaning to them. Don't forget the hostages he holds. If we tried to bring in someone from the outside to deal with them they would kill our families. We can't take the risk."

Sydney slumped in her seat. "I don't know what to do," she said. "I can't feed and care for two other people on the road. No offense, Anna, but you're an eating machine. It was hard enough for me to find food for me and Jordan. You eat as much as two or three people all by yourself."

"I'm always hungry," whined Anna. "It's not my fault."

Sydney sighed. "I know, I know—it's just how you are. I think Jordan and I could survive on the road together. He doesn't ask for much and Dogma protects us, but traveling is not an ideal lifestyle for a blind man, even one as courageous as Jordan."

Melody slid into the chair next to Sydney's and put her hand on Sydney's knee. "To take on the responsibility for another's welfare can be a terrible burden as well as a source of joy and satisfaction. When the time comes you'll know what to do. Our decisions either feel right or they feel wrong. Just keep following your heart and you'll be okay."

Sydney gave her a weak smile. "Thanks. You sound like my mother. In another life I think you and she would have been friends."

Melody smiled and stood up. "If she was anything like you, I'm sure of it. I hear a few of my four-legged patients in the barn calling me. I need to go check on them. Anna, I heard that you like animals. Why don't you come with me? Perhaps you can be of help."

After they'd gone, Sydney cleaned up the kitchen. She moved the rocking chair to the open rear window and waited for Jordan to come down for his breakfast. As she rocked she breathed in the odors of Melody's farm: sweet grass, damp dirt, and the spice from the rose bush growing against the back corner of house.

She thought about the families around Driftwood who were suffering because their loved ones were being held prisoner. It bothered her that innocent people were being starved and abused. There had to be some way to rescue them and get rid of Pharaoh and his gang.

She shook her head, her mouth twisted in a rueful expression. Sydney girl, what are you thinking? You are one woman with a blind companion and a dog. What makes you think that you can do what the entire town hasn't been able to accomplish?

The honking of a truck horn broke into her thoughts. Sydney jumped up and ran to the front window. Two men in a shiny red pickup truck were headed up the drive. They stopped outside the house and one of the men exited the truck and walked up to the house. He pounded on the front door.

"Doc! Doc, you in there? Pharaoh needs you. Doc!"

Sydney turned away from the window and quietly made her way up the stairway to the second floor. Melody's words played in her head—she did not want to become one of Pharaoh's captives. The thought of being held in a harem where men like Cal and Barrett could force their attentions on her made her want to vomit.

She rounded the corner at the top of the steps and stopped, waiting to see if the man would enter the house. The passenger shouted for Melody and pounded on the door again. Sydney peered around the corner and saw him move away from the door. She pulled back out of sight and hoped that the pounding hadn't awakened Jordan.

Several minutes passed before Sydney heard Melody return to the house. "Wait outside please. I'll just grab my medical bag and keys and I'll meet you at Pharaoh's. Can you give me some idea of the injuries so I know what to bring?"

Sydney strained to hear but the man's answer was indistinct to her ears. Melody must have walked the man away from the house.

A moment later Melody closed the front door and walked into the kitchen. "Sydney?" she called softly. "Are you here?"

Sydney poked her head around the corner and looked down the back stairs. "Up here." She kept her voice low, afraid the men would hear her. "I thought it was best to keep out of sight. What's going on?"

Melody came to the bottom of the stairs. "I have to go into town. Apparently there's been an accident and some of Pharaoh's men are hurt. It'll be safer for you to hide in the car shed after I leave in case anyone else stops by. Get Jordan up and feed him, then get Anna from the barn. I left her in the stall with the goat. She seems to like animals so she'll be okay for a little while at least. I don't know how long I'll be gone, but we'll talk more about what you should do over dinner tonight."

The front door opened and one of the men walked into the kitchen. Sydney pulled back out of his sight.

"C'mon, doc. Who you talking to? We ain't got all day. You don't want to keep Pharaoh waiting."

"Don't walk through my house in your filthy shoes! What are you, an animal? I'm talking to myself, a habit I have when I'm rushed and don't want to forget anything. I told you I'll be with you in a minute."

Sydney heard a commotion at the front door and another male voice entered the kitchen.

"Abel! What the hell's taking so long? If the doc is giving you a hard time then remind her who's boss. That husband of hers won't look so good missing an eye or an arm. Let's go —we ain't got all day."

Sydney risked a quick peek down the stairs. Her blood turned icy and her body started to tremble. She clamped her hand over her mouth to smother her gasp, and pulled back. The two men in Melody's kitchen were two of the men who had murdered Shannon. She stuffed her fist against her mouth to keep from crying out loud.

"Both of you thugs—get out of my kitchen. I said I'm coming."

Sydney heard the front door close and ran into Melody's study to watch them drive away. By angling her head she could see Melody walk to the car shed, drive the car out, and close the doors behind it.

Melody looked at the house and hitched her thumb toward the shed before she got into the car and drove off after the men.

Sydney waited until the rooster tails of dust from both vehicles disappeared before she scurried back into the hall and made her way to Jordan's room. Jordan's arm lay outside the bedsheets, exposing a well-muscled shoulder.

"Jordan! Jordan, wake up!"

Jordan's eyes flew open. He lay very still, listening.

Sydney knew he felt as disoriented as she had upon awakening in a strange room. "Jordan, it's me, Sydney. Get up and get dressed. Two men came to the house to get Melody. She had to go into town to treat some of Pharaoh's gang. She wants us to wait in the car shed until she returns."

Sydney gathered the pile of clean clothes that Melody had left for him and tossed them onto the bed. "Hurry!"

Jordan sat up, stretched his arms, and yawned as if waking in a strange bed was nothing unusual. "That was the best night's sleep I've had in years. What's your rush? The men are gone, right?"

The sheet slipped down around Jordan's hips when he sat up. Sydney stared in fascination at his bare chest, then took a hasty step away from the bed, shaken by the sudden sense of intimacy.

She had never been in a man's bedroom before. She wondered if Jordan slept naked, then flushed with embarrassment at the thought.

"The men are gone, but I recognized them, Jordan—I recognized the two men. They were part of the group who raped and killed my sister. The other ones are probably living in Driftwood now too. They all work for Pharaoh. Melody said we need to hide. What if they come back? I don't want them to find me. Get up and get dressed!"

Jordan dropped his arms and looked toward Sydney. "You never told me how your sister died. I'm so sorry, Sydney. What a horrible thing. You were lucky to escape."

A tear slid down Sydney's face. "I didn't escape. They never saw me. I was asleep in Pop's hayloft when they came and I never lifted a finger to help her. She died because of my cowardice and I'll never forgive myself. Please, Jordan, we're in danger here. We need to get out of the house."

Jordan wasn't moving. She wanted to grab his very masculine shoulders and shake some of her urgency into him but she knew Dogma wouldn't allow it.

A wrinkle appeared between Jordan's eyebrows. "Sydney, there were four of them. What could you have done? You would have ended up raped and killed like your sister. Even worse, they could have brought you to Driftwood and left you in Pharaoh's harem. You did the sensible thing, the only thing you could do. Your sister would've wanted you to survive."

"You don't understand. Shannon was my closest friend and I let her down. Can we discuss this later? If these are the kind of men that Pharaoh keeps around, then Driftwood is not a place I want to visit, let alone leave you here. We'll talk to Melody tonight and figure out where we should go. Right now I need you to get dressed and we need to get out of this house."

Jordan scowled at Sydney. His gray eyes looked into her, obviously not ready to let the argument go.

He looks right at me as if he can see everything.

"Come here. Sit." Jordan patted the bed.

"What? Jordan, I need you to get dressed. Now." Panic welled up in Sydney. She couldn't leave Jordan in the house but her need to flee was overwhelming her.

Jordan pressed his lips tight and swung his legs off the side of the bed, tucking the sheet around his hips. He reached out a foot until he felt Dogma, then bent down to scratch behind her ear. "I'm not getting dressed until you sit down." He patted the bed again and waited.

Sydney huffed a breath, then sat beside Jordan, careful not to touch him. "Satisfied? Now—Will. You. Get. Dressed?"

"Not quite. We've been together for a month now and I still have no idea what you look like. I know what you sound like—your voice is husky and warm. Sultry. I know that you smell like wildflowers and spice and the outdoors and something that is uniquely you. I want to know what you look like."

"You want me to describe myself to you? Now?" Didn't Jordan understand? They needed to get out of the house in case those men came back. She could describe herself to him later.

Jordan shook his head. "No. I want to touch your face and build a picture of you in my mind."

"If I agree, will you get dressed so we can get out of here?"

"I promise."

"Hurry up then." She held herself rigid, her face turned toward him. This close she could see tiny scars on his left temple and cheek. A thin white scar ran from his ear to his jaw. She clasped her hands together to keep from reaching up and stroking his strong, perfect jaw.

Jordan leaned close and lifted his hands to her hair. "It's so soft," he said as he gently ran his fingers through her curls. "What color is it?"

"Black." His hands felt good in her hair and she closed her eyes.

Jordan's hands cupped the sides of her head. He traced her ears with his thumbs. "Your ears are small and delicate and close to your head." His fingers were gentle as he held her head and rubbed her brow with his thumbs. He lightly felt her eyes.

The feathery touch on her eyelids tickled. A small giggle

escaped Sydney's lips. The sound startled her. When had she last laughed? Not since before her sister's death at least.

Jordan used two fingers to trace her nose. "Straight and proud, like you," he murmured. His fingers drifted lower and outlined her jaw. He rubbed his thumbs softly over her lips, outlining their shape. "Wide and generous, also like you. I can tell you're beautiful. What color is your skin?"

Sydney trembled. Jordan's exploration had left her breathless and a little dizzy.

"Always tanned-looking like my Italian mother's with green eyes. Are you ready to get dressed now?"

"Not quite." One hand slid to the back of her head and held her. The other remained lightly holding her jaw. He leaned in and softly brushed his lips against her cheek. He hesitated a moment, then pressed them firmly to her mouth.

Sydney stiffened, surprised by the kiss. Her lips tingled and a shiver ran through her body. She leaned into him and parted her lips slightly in response. She felt the cool tip of Jordan's tongue reach out to trace her bottom lip. He caught the lip gently between his teeth, then released it.

"Now I am." He grinned at her. "I've been wanting to kiss you for a while now. Thank you, Sydney."

Sydney jumped up from the bed, flustered by the kiss. Her lips still tingled and her face felt flushed. She was glad Jordan couldn't see the effect his kiss had on her.

"I'll wait in the hallway," she muttered as she made a quick exit from the bedroom.

Once in the hallway she gently touched her lips with her fingers. *Her first kiss. Oh my.*

"I'm ready, let's get out of here. Where's Anna?" Jordan came out of the bedroom with Dogma at his side. He seemed remarkably cheerful.

He also looked good in his faded jeans and chambray shirt, thought Sydney. He had rolled the cuffs up, exposing his strong, tanned forearms. Sydney again wondered how a piano player developed such a lean, muscular build, but she felt too shy to ask, especially after that kiss.

"Anna's in the barn. We'll stop by there and get her." Sydney hesitated, then took Jordan's hand and led him down the back stairs. She would not behave differently just because he had kissed her.

They were halfway across the kitchen when she heard a pickup truck come down the drive again. Sydney ran to the front window and recognized the red truck. "Oh crap, they're back. What are we going to do?"

"You're going to hide. I'll wait here and talk to them. Where's the table? Get me a cup of chicory to sit with, please, then sneak out the back door."

Sydney hesitated. She couldn't leave Jordan with the two

murderers, but she couldn't risk capture either. Duty to her friend won out. "No, we both have to run," she said.

Jordan squeezed her hand. "No. If we both run they'll catch us for sure. Besides, you know I can't run, I'm blind, remember? Now get me to the table and get out of here."

"Are you sure?" she whispered. "I-It's wrong to leave you alone with them. What if they hurt you?"

"I'll be fine. They won't kidnap me for Pharaoh's harem, but you're too beautiful for them to resist. Hurry dammit. Do as I say. I'll do my best to get rid of them."

"You think I'm beautiful?" No one had ever called Sydney beautiful before.

"Yes, I think you're beautiful. Now, will you do as I say? Please?"

Sydney led Jordan to the table and poured him a cup of chicory. She tiptoed through Melody's laundry room and opened the back door as quietly as she could. She eased out the door and closed it softly behind her. She heard the truck stop and both doors slam shut. The men were talking as they walked up the front steps.

"I'm telling you someone else is here. I thought I heard the doc talking to someone and there was a second cup on the counter. We'll just take a quick look around and then head back to town." The men entered the house without knocking.

Sydney ducked below the open kitchen window. She didn't know what Jordan had in mind, but she couldn't leave him alone with two dangerous outlaws.

"Who are you?" The voice was combative, belligerent.

"Jordan James. Who are you? Do you always enter some-one's home without knocking?"

Why did Jordan have to sound so cocky? He was going to

piss the killers off, and then they'd hurt him, or worse. A cold chill zipped down Sydney's spine.

"I'm Abel and this here's Sandman. We work for Pharaoh. What are you doing in the doc's house?"

Sydney held her breath, waiting to hear Jordan's answer.

"Just passing through. I'm an old friend of Alan's. I thought I'd stop by and see how he and Melody are doing, get a good night's sleep in a bed and a hot meal. You know how it is, traveling. Hot food's not easy to come by. The doc had to go into Driftwood to run an errand. Can I help you with anything?"

The men were silent. Sydney wanted to peek in the window but she was afraid they'd see her.

"Anyone else here?"

"Nope, just me. I'll be headed back on the road once Melody returns. Can I give her a message?"

"No. She's doctoring one of our guys who got busted up bad. Word of advice, stay out of Driftwood unless you want trouble."

Sydney breathed out a soft sigh. The men were going to leave. Then her heart stuttered. Anna's loud voice filled the kitchen.

"Hi Jordan. I got tired of waiting in the barn. Is there any oatmeal left? I'm hungry."

No! Why couldn't Anna do as she was told and stay in the barn? She was going to ruin everything.

"Good morning, Anna. I don't know about the oatmeal, you'll have to check the pot yourself."

How can he sound so calm? wondered Sydney. Her palms were perspiring. She wiped them on Melody's jeans.

"You lied to us Jordan." Abel's voice sounded tight with anger. "I asked you if there was anyone else here and you told me no. Why did you lie, Jordan?" The menace in his voice was unmistakable.

"Jordan wouldn't lie," said Anna. "I was in the barn with the goat so I wasn't here. Jordan's famous you know. He's a blind piano player."

No, Anna! Don't say anything more, please. Sydney willed Anna to be quiet but it did no good.

"He's traveled all over the world playing the piano. He can sing too. My momma and daddy had all his records. I know all the words to his songs. You can ask me, I'll sing any of them for you."

While Anna babbled on Sydney wondered what she could do to help Jordan. Should she show herself to the men? She couldn't see any way that would help the situation, but it felt wrong to let Jordan face these evil men alone. She remained where she was and prayed that Anna didn't mention her. She could hear the two men talking to each other.

"I think you'd both better come with us, James. Pharaoh will want to know about you and we don't want you taking off before he decides what to do with you. Piano man, huh? We could use some entertainment at Pharaoh's place. Good thing I came back here to check on things."

"Do you have food?" asked Anna.

Sydney almost groaned aloud. Anna didn't have a clue about the dangerous situation she had created.

"Yeah, we got food but you'll have to work for it. Shouldn't be a problem for a big girl like you. Come on piano man, get up. You're coming with us."

Sydney heard Jordan's chair scrape on the floor.

"What about my dog? She goes everywhere with me."

"No dogs. Pharaoh's got a bad association with dogs on account of he got bit by the prison guard dogs once. Anna, take hold of your friend and lead him out to the truck."

"Are you gonna give me food?"

Sydney couldn't hear the answer to Anna's question. The front door slammed. She crept to the corner of the house and peered through the rosebush. Anna was sitting in the truck's bed while Jordan sat in the rear seat. Abel turned the truck around and took off with a roar, spitting gravel from the tires. A dust cloud followed them down the road and then they were gone.

There was a moment of silence before Dogma started to howl inside the house. Sydney ran around to the front and let her out. The big dog put her nose to the ground and followed Jordan's scent to where the truck had been parked. She sat on the spot and howled again. The mournful sound ripped at Sydney's heart. She walked over to Dogma and placed her hand on the dog's large head. "Don't worry girl, we'll get him back. I promise. We'll think of something."

She stood with Dogma in the warming sun. Birds were singing, a rooster crowed. The sky stretched as far as she could see: a beautiful deep blue filled with an armada of puffy white clouds sailing east. It had started out to be a lovely day full of promise.

She had found a new friend, slept in a bed and enjoyed a hot meal. There was a chance she could leave Anna in Drift-wood. At least she was rid of Anna. But knowing that Jordan was the prisoner of a group of outlaws offset any pleasure she might have derived from losing the perpetually hungry Anna.

Sydney and Dogma remained rooted on the spot where Jordan had last stepped until Sydney spotted Melody's SUV headed toward the house.

Jordan sat behind his captors and tried to breathe shallowly. His sense of smell had sharpened after the onset of blindness and the cloud of sour body odor that filled the truck's cab made him feel ill. He thought of Sydney's enticing smell instead. He always knew when she was near because of her unique feminine scent.

If only Anna hadn't shown up. The woman was a walking catastrophe. He felt no fear for his well-being. His skill at the piano should make him useful, at least for a while. He worried about Sydney though. She had a conscience and she was a natural caretaker. She could feel obligated to try to rescue him from the Pharaoh's clutches.

He hoped Melody could make her see the futility of a rescue. She should take advantage of the situation and resume her journey to find her friend Smokey.

The thought depressed him. He had come to enjoy Sydney's company, he realized. He liked talking with her, liked walking in silence with her at his side, liked listening to her soft snores when they slept, liked waking up to her cheerful voice.

He remembered how smooth her skin had felt under his sensitive fingers. How warm and soft her lips had felt under his own. The sweet taste of her mouth…he prayed Melody would keep Sydney safe.

"What happened?" Melody stood beside Sydney and held her hand out for Dogma to sniff before patting her head.

"Those two men came back to the house and found Jordan. I hid outside. They were going to leave Jordan here—he told them he was a friend of your husband's and was just passing through—but then Anna came into the house looking for food and she told them that Jordan was a famous piano player so the men decided to take them both to Pharaoh."

Sydney's tone was flat. She stared at the road. "What am I going to do?" she asked, turning her eyes to Melody. "I don't care what happens to Anna, but I can't leave Jordan with those evil men."

Melody took Sydney's hand and gently pulled her toward the barn. "First, you're going to help me feed and doctor the animals I didn't get to this morning. Then we're going to sit down with some hot tea while you tell me exactly what happened. THEN we're going to figure out a way to get Jordan out of Pharaoh's house. Okay? Dogma, you come with us, girl. We'll get your master back, I promise."

Sydney hesitated a moment, then allowed Melody to lead her to the barn. The morning sun streamed in the big open doors and through the translucent panels over each stall. Sydney filled water buckets and forked hay into each feeder while Melody checked on the inhabitants.

The barn's pleasant, peaceful atmosphere soothed Sydney's nerves.

"Kria seems content," said Sydney, after she had fed and brushed her. "I was afraid being stalled would upset her since she's used to being outside in her own little pasture."

Melody scratched a goat kid between the ears. "Horses are social animals. They don't like to be alone at all. It depresses them. They prefer to be with other horses, but they'll befriend any animal that's available if there are no horses or ponies for them to hang with."

"Are these animals all yours?" Sydney looked at the variety of livestock in the stalls: a huge pig with a torn ear grunted at her while a swarm of piglets suckled at her teats, a mama goat stood eating while her four kids bounced around their stall, a small brown and white calf turned her warm, liquid eyes to Sydney.

The last stall held a flock of clucking hens. The hens reminded Sydney of Jordan's two chickens and she released them into an empty stall. They clucked their thanks and immediately started to peck through the bedding for insects and seeds.

"These animals all belong to the local farmers, mostly my neighbors. They're destined to end up on the table one day. This is how we manage to stay alive—we raise our own food. The farmers pay me with meat and vegetables and I provide veterinarian care when they need it."

The two women finished the chores in silence and walked back to the house. Melody made a pot of mint tea and carried the teapot and mugs into her living room. They sat together on the couch and Melody poured the tea. She handed a mug to Sydney.

"Okay, now tell me everything, please," she said, tucking her legs up underneath her body. "Don't leave anything out."

Sydney blew on her tea while she thought for a minute. "The men came back not ten minutes after you left. I recognized them. They said their names were Abel and Sandman. They were part of a gang of four men who raped and murdered my sister Shannon.

"I ran upstairs to get Jordan out of the house after you left but we weren't quick enough." She didn't mention the way Jordan had felt her face and kissed her. That was her personal secret to savor.

"They came back while we were still in the house. Jordan told me to run and hide while he stayed behind in the kitchen. He couldn't run—I hadn't thought about that. It was stupid of me."

Sydney sipped at her tea and organized her thoughts. "I

hid under the open window. Jordan acted cool and collected, like he belonged here. He never let on that he was blind. He told them he was a friend of your husband's and they bought his story. They were going to leave him here because he told them he was leaving today. Then Anna came into the house looking for food and told them Jordan was a famous blind piano player. They were mad because he had lied to them and they took Jordan and Anna to Pharaoh's. They said Pharaoh could use an entertainer."

Melody didn't say anything for several minutes while she drank her tea. Finally she set her cup down. "First, I'm sorry to hear about your sister, Sydney. That was a terrible thing for them to do and even worse for you to witness. I'm not surprised by what they did. Abel and Sandman are brutal men. Sandman got his name because he likes to put people to sleep—permanently."

"You were right to hide today. You can't help Jordan if you've been captured too. I'm sure he'll be all right, at least for a while, until the novelty of having an entertainer wears off. They might abuse him, but they won't kill him. I imagine they'll put Anna to work, so she'll be okay."

"I don't care about Anna. She's a horrible person and I'm glad to be rid of her." Anna had been nothing but trouble since Sydney tried to rescue her. She hoped she never saw the woman again.

Melody nodded. "I can see why you'd feel that way, but Anna carries her own burdens, just like the rest of us. Life hasn't been easy for her and she finds solace in eating. She was a big help to me in the barn. I think she could be trained to be a veterinarian's assistant. She's certainly strong enough and she loves animals."

"I watched her kill one man and badly injure another when they tried to attack Dogma. Anna went berserk; it was scary. I never want that anger directed at me. Sometimes, when I wouldn't give her my food, I thought she might attack and kill me too."

Dogma padded across the floor from the window where she had been staring toward the road and sat next to Sydney. She lowered her head to Sydney's knees and focused her golden eyes on her face. Sydney rubbed her ear. She didn't need Melody to tell her what Dogma was thinking.

"How are we going to get Jordan out of Pharaoh's place?" she asked quietly. "I refuse to leave him there. Your neighbors have been powerless against the guy. He can't imprison one of my family members to control me, but I'm only one person. I can't fight him alone."

"I gave the problem some thought while we were in the barn," replied Melody. "I think perhaps the time has come for us to do something about Pharaoh and his men and take back our town. It won't be easy and people may die, but today I realized that I don't want to spend the rest of my life living in constant fear. Pharaoh's prisoners are starved and beaten until they die. He'll never let any of them go free. We need to find a way to rid ourselves of the evil in this town."

Melody stood up from the couch in one smooth movement. "Come on, let's talk to the neighbors and see how many people we can round up to help. It shouldn't be too hard to convince most of them—we all have a family member in Pharaoh's jail that we'd like to save."

Melody led Sydney to a small shed behind the house and unlocked it. She wheeled out two knobby-tired mountain bikes, leaned them against the shed, and checked the tires. "Good to go," she said, straightening up. "Glad I kept these around."

"Bicycles? Why don't we just take the SUV? It'll be faster."

"Because Pharaoh checks my mileage every week. He

recharges the SUV at his place so I can tend to his gang, and for no other purpose. If I travel somewhere that is unauthorized he hurts Alan. I learned that the hard way. So we bike or we walk, which will take far longer. Mount up." Melody took the men's bike and left the women's for Sydney.

It had been many years since Sydney had ridden a bicycle. Melody was halfway down the drive before Sydney had even figured out the gears. "Wait for me!" she hollered.

Melody turned around and waved at her. "Hurry up slowpoke, we don't have all day you know."

Sydney pumped the pedals and caught up with the older woman. Dogma trotted at their side, tongue lolling out the side of her mouth. She looked happy to be moving again.

They turned in at the first farm, a small operation a mile beyond Melody's place. Flocks of chickens roamed the yard scratching for insects and fresh green shoots.

"This is the Simon's place. Pharaoh has their fourteen-year-old son Brent," explained Melody as they leaned the bicycles against the front porch. She ran up the steps and knocked on the door.

A middle-aged woman cracked open the door barely wide enough to see who was knocking. Deep furrows ran beside her mouth and her eyes were tired and lined. It was a look Sydney grew accustomed to as she and Melody met with people throughout the day.

"Hi Mary Ann, this is my friend Sydney Waters. We need to talk with you and Henry. Is he around?"

Mary Ann looked at Melody for a moment, silent, and then opened the door to admit them. "I'll get him. Go on through to the kitchen."

Melody and Sydney met with ten families before they had to return to Melody's place. At first the families were reluctant to even discuss the possibility of taking on Pharaoh and his men, afraid that their loved ones would be punished, or worse, killed, but as Melody talked they began to gain support.

"Why'd we quit? We were doing great," asked Sydney as they put the bicycles back inside the shed.

"I have to go back into town to check on Pharaoh's injured men. This won't happen overnight, Sydney. It will take time to get everyone organized and to work out a solid plan of attack. Now that I'm thinking about it, having to check on Pharaoh's men will give me an excuse to gather useful information."

Melody patted Sydney's arm. "Not to worry," she said. "We'll get your friends back, and our families as well. We made a good start today. I wasn't sure if people would agree with our idea, but they are as fed up as I am with the situation. The families we talked with today are going to contact others and we'll all meet up at Thorson's barn in two day's time. That will give me a chance to see what we're up against at Pharaoh's."

"I know you all have a lot at stake. I'm just worried about Jordan." Sydney didn't want Anna back, but she didn't want to argue with Melody about it. Melody held a higher opinion of Anna than she did, and Sydney knew Melody would insist on rescuing Anna also.

"Your friends will be fine for a while. I'll check on Jordan today, I promise. Perhaps you could feed and water the animals for me while I run into town. I shouldn't be too long, but it will be safer for you to wait in the barn until I return."

22

SYDNEY AND DOGMA were curled up together napping in an empty stall when she heard someone enter the barn. She got to her knees and started to call out, but stopped when she saw that Dogma was on the alert. Whoever had entered the barn was not Melody.

Sydney crawled under the stall's wall feeder and pressed her body against the aisle wall. If anyone looked, they wouldn't be able to see her unless they entered the stall.

"I'm telling you, the doc is hiding someone else."

Sydney recognized Sandman's voice. She squeezed herself into a smaller ball and pressed her face to her knees.

"That girl Anna that we picked up this morning mentioned someone named Sydney, and Rob said he had captured an exotic beauty to bring to Pharaoh, but she escaped when Anna attacked him."

Rob! He was alive! Somehow he had survived and made his way to Driftwood. A thin layer of cold sweat broke out on Sydney's back. They knew about her and they were here looking for her. That imbecile Anna couldn't keep her mouth shut. If she were here right now Sydney would gladly run her through with a pitchfork.

"She's not in the house or the shed. Start checking the stalls. I know she's hiding here somewhere. I wouldn't mind getting my hands on her and having a little fun before we bring her to the boss."

Sydney heard Sandman enter the first stall in the same aisle where she was hiding. There was no way out. If she left the stall they would see her and she knew she couldn't outrun them. If she stayed, Sandman would reach her stall within a few minutes. Fear pooled in her belly. She squeezed her eyes shut and prayed.

Sandman opened and checked the five stalls between the door and the stall where Sydney crouched under the feeder. Abel searched the stalls in the opposite aisle, keeping pace with Sandman.

Sydney heard Sandman's steps approach and stop at her stall door. She waited to feel his hands grab her and pull her from her hiding spot. The stall door began to slide open. Dogma emitted a low, menacing growl and bared her teeth.

"Shit! There's a monster dog in this stall!" Sandman slid the stall shut with a bang. "No way anyone could hide in there with that beast. Let's get out of here. The girl is gone. She probably left when we took her friends away. We'll drive the roads around Driftwood—she can't have walked far."

Sydney waited until she heard the big doors slam shut, then uncurled her body. She threw her arms around Dogma's neck and buried her face in the dog's fur. "Thank you, girl. That's the second time you've saved my life."

They remained in the barn until Melody returned several hours later. She checked the animals that needed medical attention before they headed into the house, refusing to talk about her trip to Pharaoh's until she had made some hot food and they both sat down to eat.

"Okay, now will you tell me what's going on?" Sydney asked after she gathered up their empty dishes and set them in the sink. Melody gave a tired sigh and Sydney felt a stab of guilt—the doc had put in a long, hard day and had to be exhausted.

"Let's go sit on the couch so you can put your feet up," suggested Sydney in a kinder tone.

"Thank you, I am tired, I have to admit."

When they were settled in the living room Sydney looked at Melody expectantly. "Okay, spill. How's Jordan doing?"

Melody chuckled. "Better than us, believe it or not. Pharaoh is impressed with Jordan's international celebrity status and is treating him like royalty. He's given Jordan a private suite and had a grand piano brought into the mansion and set up in the ballroom. Jordan was being served dinner while I was there, so they wouldn't let me talk with him, but I saw him. Pharaoh had him dressed in a tux. He looked very handsome. I made sure Jordan could hear my voice, so he knows I was there."

Sydney blew out some of the tension she had been holding. "I'm so relieved. I'd feel awful if they hurt him."

Melody gave her a searching look. "You care about him."

Sydney looked at her and blushed. "Well, sure, of course I do. I feel responsible for him. Besides, he kind of grows on you. Jordan's good company—he's interesting and entertaining and he has a great sense of humor."

To stop any more probing, she changed the subject. "Did you gather any useful info about Pharaoh's place that will help us?"

"I did. I'll draw up a floor plan and mark where his men

live. As near as I can tell, there are close to thirty of them living in the house."

"Thirty! *And* a ballroom? How big is this place?"

"Palatial. The building belongs in Driftwood about as well as a tree frog in the desert. Having money doesn't necessarily mean one has good taste." She stopped to rub her feet and groaned.

Sydney practiced patience, but it wasn't easy. Her hands itched to wring everything the doc had learned from her throat.

"The good news is that Pharaoh has grown complacent," Melody continued. "There were only four watchmen posted outside. He believes we won't attack him as long as he holds our families hostage, and he has relaxed his guard considerably. Most of his men were partying inside the house, waiting for Jordan to entertain them. Our attack will be a genuine surprise."

They washed the dinner dishes and made their way upstairs. Sydney watched Dogma sniff Jordan's empty bed with a lump in her throat. Would she see him again? She took Dogma into her room and scratched the dog's ears and chest and whispered to her that she would do her best to return Jordan to her soon.

The wait until the meeting seemed interminable. Melody and Sydney pedaled the bicycles against a dry, irritating wind to the Thorson farm. A long, white dairy barn stood behind the Thorson's farmhouse. At first Sydney thought no one else had shown up, but upon entering the barn she found a crowd standing quietly, waiting for her and Melody to arrive. Most had walked, some had ridden bicycles or horses.

Everything was crowded inside the barn so there would be no outward sign of the assembly on the off-chance Pharaoh's men did a drive-by.

Melody started the meeting with the information that she had gathered over the previous two days. Ideas were tossed out, argued over, and discarded. These people were farmers, not soldiers, and it soon became apparent to Sydney that they were unsure of themselves when it came to planning a turf war.

Finally an elderly man sporting a white ponytail limped forward and the crowd quieted. His demeanor and the people's reaction to him told Sydney that he was a respected member of the community. She hoped he had something to contribute because the group had made no progress after two hours of talk.

His voice was surprisingly strong coming from someone who looked as old as her grandfather. Although he walked with a cane, closer inspection told Sydney that the man was not as elderly as she had first assumed. Someone in the crowd addressed him as Captain and her hopes soared—perhaps this man had combat experience.

"What do we have for weapons?" he asked.

"Nothing—Pharaoh's men took all our guns," answered someone from the rear of the assembly.

Sydney raised her hand. "I have a small crossbow, a sling-shot, and several knives."

The Captain turned intelligent brown eyes to her and he nodded in approval. "Very good. We have to think beyond guns. Anyone else?"

People spoke over each other as they came up with a list of possible weapons from their farms: pitchforks, iron bars, scythes, shovels, tire irons, chains, clubs. The Captain nodded and smiled at each contributor while Melody made a list.

When the last item had been noted the Captain raised his hand for their attention. "It seems to me that our first priority must be our family members. We need to release them from the barn where they are being held so there can be no retaliation. Once we accomplish that we release the women and girls from the harem. Only then can we move on Pharaoh and his men. Agreed?"

Everyone gave their assent.

"Excellent. We need more intelligence on the barn where they're holding the prisoners. Is anyone scheduled for a visit this week?"

Several people raised their hands. Sydney learned that Pharaoh only allowed a single family member into the prison-barn at a time to keep the guards from being outnumbered. Because the prisoners were never released from their shackles, no more than three guards were needed to watch over them.

"What do we do about the guards?" The speaker was a short, rotund man with a bald head and a neatly trimmed beard.

Despite a lack of razor blades, Sydney noted that all the men present kept their facial hair neat. These were people who continued to take pride in their farms and their appearance despite the challenging circumstances. It was a small thing, but it boosted her confidence in them. Pharaoh may have the upper hand, but these people hadn't given up.

"Does anyone have any ideas about how to immobilize the guards?" The Captain looked around the barn.

There was murmuring but no one spoke up. After several minutes a plump, rosy-cheeked woman raised her hand.

"Yes, Althea. Do you have an idea?" asked the Captain.

Althea's face turned deep red. "Whenever I try to bring one of my pies in to my boy, Thomas, the guards take it for themselves. What if we lace it with a strong laxative? I think I still have some left from when I bred Himalayan cats. They were always getting hairballs so I had to give them the squirts every now and then to keep their digestive systems working."

No one said anything for a moment. Sydney imagined everyone was picturing hairballs and cats with diarrhea. She stifled a giggle.

"I can work out a dosage that will hit them hard and fast," said Melody. "It's not foolproof, but chances are good that it will at least slow them down so we can incapacitate them."

The group joked and laughed about how the guards deserved what was coming to them. The Captain let them go on for several minutes before calling them to order again.

He lost his grin and grew serious. "That brings us to Pharaoh and his posse. It will be near impossible to over-come them without bloodshed. We need to be prepared to do whatever is necessary to incapacitate them. Once we start this war, we'll have to finish it. That means that we may have to kill, or worse, some of us may be killed."

No one spoke. Everyone knew that their imprisoned family members would pay with their lives if they failed.

"Why don't we use the laxative trick on them as well?" The speaker was a whip-thin, white-haired man with piercing blue eyes.

Sydney realized that most of the crowd was older, past middle age. She was the youngest adult there. Apparently Pharaoh had locked up or killed anyone young enough to be a threat.

"No, it's too iffy for a large group, Jonah," replied the Captain. "We can be relatively sure the three guards will all partake of Althea's pie, but we have no way to dose Pharaoh and his men. We need something more foolproof for them."

"We have someone on the inside at Pharaoh's," said Melody. "Two people, altho one is blind. We know a young woman working in Pharaoh's kitchen. She's a friend of my house guest, Sydney, and she has no relatives in the prison so it won't hurt her to help us."

"That may be, but what can she do? Poison them? Are we all going to become murderers?" The question came from a florid-faced man toward the back of the barn.

Melody shrugged her shoulders. "I don't know, Terry. I'm thinking out loud, hoping it will stimulate some ideas. We'll do whatever we have to do. Pharaoh doesn't hesitate to kill one of our loved ones if it suits him, I think we have to go into this with the same mindset."

"I will not become a murderer, even to save my son. Killing is plain wrong, it says so in the ten commandments. Or have you forgotten your religion, Melody?"

Melody flushed but stood her ground. "That's a low blow, Terry. We all do what we have to do. In my mind, leaving Alan to rot away in a cell until he dies when I can do something about it amounts to murder as well. A murder of neglect, but it's still murder. I'd rather have the death of an evil man on my hands than the death of my husband."

Quiet murmurs of agreement rippled through the group.

Sydney was growing tired of standing. It felt as if they had been there for half the night and were making very little progress. She shuffled her feet and tried to stretch her muscles without being obvious. An idea popped into her mind.

"What about a tranquilizer?" She turned to Melody. "You're a vet, you must have something you use for large animals. We could get Anna to put it into their dinner: a pot of soup, or a stew, something that would disguise the taste. It might not knock them all out completely, but it would slow down their reflexes depending on how much they ate. At least we'd have a fighting chance. With a tranquilizer we might be able to capture them and return them to jail without any killing."

The Captain smiled at Sydney and she felt a small flush of pleasure. "That's a great idea, young lady. Doc, is it feasible?"

"I'll have to check my supplies, but yes, it could work," said Melody. "If anyone has any sedatives left bring them to me. I'll pool what we have and see if it's enough."

The remainder of the night was spent hashing out the details of who would be responsible for what. By the time the meeting adjourned with plans to meet again in another three day's time, Sydney barely had the energy to pedal back to Melody's place.

The doc seemed unfazed by the late hour. She talked excitedly as they rode home, energized by the hope that she might see her husband freed.

Sydney pedaled silently through the starry night, barely registering Melody's words. Her nightmares grew more vivid with each passing day. Last night she had awakened drenched in sweat, trembling, with the image of Barrett's smashed skull and staring dead eye etched in her mind.

She held a key role in the attack on Pharaoh. The only person with a weapon that could be used at a distance, she had been assigned the task of taking out the four house guards with her crossbow pistol. The Captain would produce a new supply of arrows for her, and Melody was concocting a numbing agent for the arrows.

More deaths on her hands. Would there ever be an end to them? If she was destined to become a killer why couldn't she have started sooner and saved Shannon? Sydney missed her sister with a fierceness that frightened her. She wondered if the wound of her loss would ever heal.

She pedaled harder, wiped her tears on her sleeve, and forced her thoughts back to the present.

Her only choices were to run away and leave the people of Driftwood to deal with Pharaoh's gang without her, or to travel farther down the road to hell. If she ran away she would be abandoning Jordan in the same way she had abandoned Shannon.

Her parents had taught her to respect the sanctity of life. Smokey had taught her that every living thing had value and was part of the Creator. What right did she have to destroy another's life? Did the fact that Pharaoh and his men were killers change things?

A cold, hard lump of determination settled in Sydney's chest. She would do what she had to do. If she survived, she would find Smokey and confess her sins.

If she survived.

Odds were she would end up sacrificing her life in the attack on Pharaoh. She marveled at how calm she felt about facing her own death. She was prepared to die to atone for the lives she had destroyed.

No one escaped the wheel of karma, and she owed a heavy debt—a debt that would soon become far heavier. It was a burden she could not carry for long without going crazy.

Death would be a welcome release.

THE NEXT THREE days passed quickly. Sydney helped Melody with her animal patients and practiced shooting her crossbow at a paper silhouette shaped like a man.

Despite her skill with the crossbow, her first few shots went far wide of the paper human target. The idea of intentionally shooting a human made Sydney ill.

Her hand trembled as she raised and aimed her crossbow pistol. She jerked the gun to the right at the moment she let the arrow fly.

She reminded herself that Pharaoh was a criminal, his men rapists and murderers. She stoked the fires of her anger until gradually she was able to aim at the target's legs and arms.

By day three she looked at the target with cold dispassion and placed her arrows in the heart region of the silhouette.

She spent her free time in bed reading from Melody's library, but mostly staring at the ceiling and thinking about life and death and karma. Why did so many good people have to suffer?

The people she'd met through the doc were decent, hard-working farmers, not criminals. Why were their innocent children being made to suffer at the hands of the bad guys?

None of it made any sense. If there was truly a Creator he had messed up bad. His law of karma was not working. And if there was no law of karma, then what code of behavior could she base her life on? Why would anyone strive to be good if the bad always won?

She felt as if all the joy and wonder she felt for the beauty in the world had drained from her soul leaving nothing but a lump of black ice. Nothing but death.

On the third day the final meeting took place soon after dark in Thorson's barn.

Sydney felt the change in the atmosphere right away. The people stood taller, seemed more energized and more focused. Despair had been banished by hope.

She heard very little conversation. Everything had been discussed and decided upon—there was nothing left to say. They were ready for action.

The Captain looked like a professional soldier dressed in camouflage fatigues. She was surprised to see that he had cut his ponytail off. With his hair cut close to his scalp he looked years younger and more like a military leader.

Sydney looked around the barn and realized that nearly everyone had made a similar change. Hair and beards were trimmed short, hunting clothes had been aired out and repaired. No one wore the traditional hunter's bright orange: they were all dressed for stealth in dark wool and camouflage patterned jackets and pants—even the women.

The Captain called the meeting to order.

Before the Captain could say anything further, the man

called Terry, now wearing a cleric's collar, pushed forward. "I need to speak my piece, Captain."

Terry turned and faced his neighbors. "I implore you all to think about what you are doing. If anyone dies at your hands you will pay a dear price. Your souls will rot in hell. Killing is wrong, there is no justification for it, no matter what Doc Hebrig says. Anyone who agrees should leave with me now and not be a part of this."

The preacher made his way toward the door. No one followed. He stopped and turned back, lifted his hands, palms up. His expression turned beseeching. "Last chance people, I beg you to reconsider. I cannot give you my blessing on this. You'll be on your own."

No one moved.

"I'd rather be a sinner then let my Jeb rot in that filthy barn any longer," said a stocky brown-haired woman. "You don't have family, Reverend. You don't understand. We have to do this, no matter the price."

The others murmured in agreement.

Terry lowered his hands. "So be it. You will all be condemned as sinners." He left the barn.

The Captain took control of the meeting and went over the final plan one last time to be sure everyone knew what was expected of them. Some things had to be left to chance. Would the three men guarding the barn eat the pie containing the laxative? Would Anna put the sedative in the stew? The success of the attack depended upon those two events happening.

At the end of the meeting the Captain looked each one in the eye. "This won't be easy, and some of us may be seriously injured or even killed. I believe we have a good plan and a good chance to make it work. I want every one of you to know that I'm proud of you and proud to fight alongside you for the lives of our loved ones. Go home and try to rest, we move on Pharaoh and his gang at sunset tomorrow. It could be a long night."

Melody and Sydney rode back to the farm in silence. Too keyed up to crawl into bed, they settled on the couch with mugs of hot tea.

"Who is the Captain?" asked Sydney. "I thought he was elderly at first, but now he seems closer to your age even with that white hair."

Melody rested her head against the back of the couch. "His name is John Templeton. He was a Captain in the Marine Corps. Maybe still is. I don't know if the armed services still exist to be honest. It doesn't matter, we call John 'Captain' out of respect for his service to our country."

"Did he injure his leg in a war?" Sydney wasn't really that curious about the Captain but she didn't want to talk about what lay ahead of them. Dogma wandered over and sat against Sydney's legs. She leaned down and pressed her cheek to the top of the dog's large head.

"No. Pharaoh did that. John tried to stop Pharaoh from taking his wife and fifteen year old daughter. Naomi was a beautiful woman and Karen looks just like her. Pharaoh smashed John's leg with a maul while several of his men held John down."

Sydney noticed the tremble in Melody's hand as she brought the mug of tea to her mouth. "You don't have to tell me anymore if it's too difficult." Her mouth felt dry and she wished she hadn't asked about the Captain. Somehow she knew she didn't want to hear his story, it was going to be too painful.

"Naomi and Karen were Pharaoh's first victims. They grabbed them while they were in town picking up supplies. Pharaoh's men held John while they raped and murdered

Naomi. They took his daughter for Pharaoh's harem and told us they would do the same to every female in the county if anyone tried to retaliate for their actions. For a long while we didn't think John would ever recover. His hair turned white practically overnight."

"Pharaoh deserves to die." Sydney's voice was barely a whisper.

"I agree." Melody sounded calm, matter of fact. "Some men are too evil to be allowed to live."

"Can that be true?" asked Sydney. "I worry about karma. Killing is wrong, but at times it seems necessary. I can't reconcile the two."

Melody shrugged and set her mug on the coffee table. "I don't worry about it. We do what we have to do. I've never killed and I don't go looking for people to kill, but I believe that if I had to take a life to save another, I would. That's the best I can do."

She said that so easily, but she'd never killed, thought Sydney. Melody had no idea what it was like to take a life. Sydney had killed two men. What does that make her? Would her soul rot in hell like Terry the preacher said?

Sydney couldn't voice her thoughts aloud to Melody—she knew the woman wouldn't understand why Sydney felt so troubled. She had killed to save her grandfather—and herself, if she was completely honest. The murders were justified. Or were they?

Was murder ever justified or was all life sacred no matter the circumstances?

The battle in her heart felt as if she was being ripped into pieces. A large part held nothing but anger and death. But she realized she still had a tiny piece of hope that all life mattered, that there was order in the universe, that love and karma ultimately trumped all.

Sydney took Dogma outside for a short walk, then crawled into her bed. She didn't expect to sleep and was surprised when the sound of Melody's SUV woke her the next morning.

———

The plan was in motion. The day had passed too quickly for Sydney. It was now late afternoon and Althea should be delivering her pie to the unsuspecting guards.

Sydney took a long, steamy shower. She knew that Melody would prefer cold water over having to doctor Pharaoh's men, but at the moment Sydney was grateful for the hot water. She felt certain this would be her last shower and she savored every moment.

She didn't expect to survive the battle tonight. Her only responsibility was neutralizing the four house guards, but she had decided to join the battle and fight until the end.

Once she killed the four guards she would have six murders on her hands. What were a few more? Her karma was already screwed—she may as well do everything she could to help Melody's friends take back their town.

She dressed carefully in brown and tan camo-patterned pants, a dark brown shirt, and her mother's hiking boots. She dug into her pack and pulled a dainty, pale blue handkerchief from the depths. She carefully unfolded the handkerchief and lifted the blue enamel bluebird from its folds. Once belonging to her grandmother, the bluebird pin had been a favorite of Shannon's. Sydney rubbed its smooth surface against her lips and pinned it to her shirt collar.

She fastened the knife sheath to her thigh, set her father's crusher hat on her head and tied a bandana to her belt loop in honor of Smokey, who always carried a bandana. She would carry her grandfather's ironwood staff along with her other weapons. Something of everyone she loved would accompany her into battle.

Sydney ate several bowls of the stew Melody had left bubbling on the stove for her. She felt strangely calm, her mind mercifully blank. She had expected to be shaky and nervous, but now that the time had come she felt detached from the whole affair, more like an observer rather than a participant.

The setting sun painted the sky a garish rose and purple-gray in honor of the coming battle. Flocks of blackbirds headed for their evening roost wheeled and darted in the sky. Stars began to glitter in the gathering dark to the east.

Everyone was in place. Sydney and Melody waited in the front seats of Melody's SUV. The Captain sat in the back seat along with two other men. Dogma occupied the cargo section.

Sydney wanted Dogma on hand for Jordan and had insisted that Melody bring her. She knew that Dogma would take care of Jordan no matter what happened. Dogma was Jordan's best, and maybe only, chance of survival.

They were parked just west of town, near the dairy barn that housed Pharaoh's prisoners, waiting for word from Althea. The others stood nearby in the shadow of Driftwood's water tower.

Sydney welcomed the light breeze that blew off the river through the open windows. No one made a sound. Even Dogma panted in silence.

Althea came around the end of the barn and raised both hands to the sky.

"There's Althea's signal. Frank, take your group and secure the barn." The Captain spoke quietly. Frank exited the

SUV and gathered several men from the group waiting under the water tower, then headed toward the barn.

The wait seemed to last forever, but Sydney knew it couldn't have been longer than ten minutes before the large doors at the south end of the barn rolled open.

She heard a collective sigh from the group standing under the water tower. Sydney, Melody, and the Captain climbed out of the SUV and joined the others as they quickly made their way to the barn.

The guards lay on the ground near the open doors, hands and feet tightly bound, mouths gagged. One moaned and a nasty stench rose from his pants.

"Now you assholes know what it feels like to lie in your own filth." Althea's eyes glinted with satisfaction. She walked over to Sydney. "Brace yourself, Sydney What you are about to see would make even the most unfeeling man weep."

Sydney stopped inside the wide barn doors and waited for her eyes to adjust to the gloom. A vile odor reached her nose and she opened her mouth to breathe, willing herself not to be sick. She smelled manure, ammonia, rotted garbage, and death. Someone brought a pair of lanterns into the barn and lit them.

At first she didn't understand the tableau revealed by the lanterns. She moved into the center aisle of the dairy barn. Rows of milking machinery ran down both side aisles. She strained to see better and stepped closer to the aisle on her right.

A pile of rags lay in the compacted manure. Sydney jumped and uttered a faint scream when the rags moved. Then she saw the ropes that lashed the rags to the milking apparatus.

Oh my god. Horror gripped her. These were the prisoners. She pulled her knife from the sheath and stepped closer to the rag pile.

"My name is Sydney," she said gently. "I'm going to cut these ropes. I'll try not to hurt you." She noticed the raw skin on the prisoner's bony wrists and did her best not to let the ropes rub against them. She severed the ropes and gently lowered the prisoner's arms.

Sydney looked around for the Captain and saw him working across the center aisle in the opposite milking stall.

"Captain, what should I do? I'm afraid to move…" Sydney hesitated. The body at her feet was caked with filth and so emaciated she had no idea if it was a male or female. "…this person," she finished lamely.

"Concentrate on cutting them free. The others will carry them outside." He gently lifted the body at his feet and carried it out of the barn, crooning soft words to the sagging body in his arms.

Sydney spent the next half hour hacking through ropes. Most of the prisoners were too weak to speak, although several opened their eyes and looked at her with haunted expressions. Two of the people she freed turned out to be dead. All but two, Melody's husband Alan and another young man, were children and teens.

Sydney walked out of the barn after releasing the last prisoner and searched for Melody. She found the doc holding a canteen of water to a young girl's lips.

"I'll stay here with a few of the mothers and start cleaning these children up. We brought clean clothing for everyone."

"Not everyone made it." Grief for the unknown victims filled Sydney. She pushed down the tears that threatened to spill.

"I know, John told me." The canteen shook in Melody's hand. "It's selfish of me, but I'm relieved that Alan survived.

John wants you to meet him at the SUV. The others are already headed to Pharaoh's."

Sydney looked at the starved and filthy bodies laying about her and let go of any remaining guilt over killing Pharaoh and his men.

24

JORDAN RAN his fingers lightly over the familiar ivory keys. He knew this piece by heart and allowed his attention to drift. He had been at Pharaoh's nearly a week now and the monotony was beginning to get to him. Every night followed the same routine: he played light classical during dinner, then moved into rock and jazz for the inevitable party that followed.

He couldn't complain about his host's hospitality. He had been housed in a private two room suite with full bath and maid service. Pharaoh had even located a grand piano and had it moved here for him.

Jordan suspected they were in a ballroom. He could tell by the way the music echoed that the room was as large as some of the venues he had played as a professional.

He finished the piece and inclined his head slightly to acknowledge the smattering of applause. He adjusted his tails and began another piece that required little of his attention. Pharaoh had turned Driftwood upside down until he dug up several tuxedos that fit Jordan as if they were made especially for him.

Jordan appreciated the gesture, but would have preferred to play in jeans. Wearing a tux for this group of half-wits felt wrong. He suspected that Pharaoh's men would just as soon kill him as listen to classical music, but they did as they were told.

Jordan smelled beef stew and his stomach growled. He wouldn't be fed until the party ended, sometimes not until early dawn. This was Pharaoh's version of "singing for his supper" and a reminder to Jordan that he was Pharaoh's prisoner and under his control.

He focused on the room to take his mind off the gnawing hunger. He located the half dozen round tables scattered along the windowed wall to his right and fixed the location of each in his mind.

With nothing to do but wait for Pharaoh's summons, he had been honing his radar skills. He knew the opposite wall was mostly windows. The piano notes bounced more sharply off glass than they did wood or plasterboard. He wondered what view the house builder had chosen and if the sun had set yet.

Male voices rose and fell, laughed and argued. Arguing seemed to be a favorite pastime of Pharaoh's crew. Fights broke out almost every night and were encouraged. The men constantly jockeyed for position within the gang, especially those high up in the organization.

Jordan focused on the different voices. He counted twenty-seven, including Pharaoh's deep bass. Ten men were missing. Those would be the various guards.

He knew from talking with his maid that four men always guarded the outside of the house, two men guarded the harem prisoners, one watched the kitchen, and three stood guard on the barn of prisoners that Doc Melody had mentioned.

He heard Pharaoh's voice go flat and soft. Uh-oh. Someone had better watch out. Jordan recognized the warning in Pharaoh's tone and knew Pharaoh wouldn't hesitate to punish the offender for his crime, imagined or real.

Pharaoh ruled through fear and physical might, and this crowd of gangsters needed constant reminding of who sat in the boss's chair.

Penny, his maid, told him that Pharaoh had killed one of his top men just last week for helping himself to a girl from Pharaoh's harem. She confided that the harem consisted of the prettiest local girls and young women kidnapped from their families solely for Pharaoh's use.

When Jordan asked Penny if she had been part of the harem, she told him she was too plain looking. The wistfulness in Penny's voice prompted Jordan to take her hand and tell her that physical beauty was only a shallow veneer—it was the beauty a person carried inside that counted.

He told her he could tell that she possessed a great deal of internal beauty. Since that day, Penny had dropped her timid shell. She showed greater confidence in Jordan's presence and began to share the goings-on of Pharaoh's men.

Jordan wondered how long he had before Pharaoh grew bored with his music. For the moment he was a novelty that added class to Pharaoh's reputation, but when the novelty wore off he felt sure he would be disposed of.

Pharaoh summoned Jordan to his private quarters every afternoon to hear stories about his concert tours and the famous people he met and played for. Jordan soon realized that Pharaoh was starstruck, a secret groupie with an unquenchable thirst for gossip about movie stars and other musicians. He began to embellish his accounts and even lie outright to feed Pharaoh's insatiable appetite for the "inside" scoop.

Jordan felt a little like the male version of Queen Scheherazade—as long as he could entertain Pharaoh with different stories he would be allowed to live.

He moved onto a Mozart sonata, and as they often did, his thoughts drifted to Sydney. Where was she now? Had she continued her journey to find her friend Smokey? Jordan felt the familiar pang of jealousy that hit him whenever he imagined Sydney with the mysterious Smokey.

Sydney was the only friend he had made since becoming blind. His young friends had deserted him after the accident —afraid of his affliction and warned not to speak of all the things that Jordan could no longer do, they hadn't known how to act around him anymore and so had drifted off.

He didn't blame them; when you're seven what is there to talk about besides sports and video games and television? All activities that required two working eyes, which he no longer possessed.

Jordan missed Sydney's scent and her sultry contralto voice. He missed her enthusiasm and the way she described the world as they passed through it, the way she appreciated every little flower and insect.

He remembered how her strong fingers felt entwined with his, and the way her face felt under his fingers. He wished he could see her—he knew she possessed beauty inside and out, no matter how she denied it.

He thought of how her mouth felt under his own, warm and generous and soft and inviting. What he wouldn't give to kiss her again.

Sydney also possessed a sadness that she tried to keep hidden from him, but he could sense it in her and ached to be the one to banish it.

She had told him about her sister Shannon's rape and murder, and he knew Shannon's death haunted her, but there was something more, something insidious that was eating away at her soul. He felt the dark waves of despair seep off her when they slept side by side and her nightmares took hold.

His fingers grew still on the piano keys as a sharp pang of loneliness tore through him. He took a deep, shuddering breath and pushed it down.

Sydney was safe, nothing else mattered. His life was here now, for as long as it lasted. He would cherish his memories of the young woman who had dared to broaden his world and be happy that she had escaped Pharaoh's clutches.

Jordan began to play a complicated piece that demanded his attention. It was time to set aside his memories until later when he was alone in his room and could savor them.

Sydney crouched behind the chest-high stone wall that surrounded Pharaoh's estate and examined the front of the house that sprawled over the once-manicured grounds. It was the largest private home she had ever seen. The Captain told her the house had been built by a Mr. Fred Leighton, owner of Driftwood Beef Processing, now deceased at the hands of Pharaoh.

The center portion of the house consisted of an imposing three stories of brick and glass. Long, two-story wings extended off both sides. According to Melody, the wing to the west housed Pharaoh's private quarters and his harem.

Jordan slept on the first floor of the east wing along with the higher-up men in Pharaoh's organization. The remaining men slept on the upper floors of the two wings.

Sydney circled around to the back of the house, careful to keep below the wall. Even though it was nearly full dark, the house had power and outside lights. The lights were aimed toward the house, more for theatrics than security, but she didn't want to risk discovery.

She had been surprised to learn that Pharaoh's place had electricity, a rare commodity in today's world. Driftwood possessed a generating dam on the river that had escaped damage when the devastating quakes destroyed most of the world's power sources.

The Captain told her that when Pharaoh took control of the town he ordered the power cut to everywhere that wasn't essential to him. The dam's operating engineer had no choice but to obey when a member of his family was taken hostage.

Sydney reached the back of the house. The grounds dropped away from the house here and sloped down to the Missouri River. The lowest level of the house, invisible in the front, opened onto the yard in the rear. The kitchens and servant quarters were located on the below ground level.

From her vantage point Sydney could see gleaming appliances and people moving around in the kitchen. She took out her binoculars and looked for Anna. She found her seated at a long table, eating. That figured.

The level above the kitchen held the ballroom. She heard faint notes from a piano and male voices through the glass wall that looked over the rear grounds. Upward-facing wall sconces cast a soft light over the room.

Sydney shifted the binoculars to inspect the ballroom. Six tables. Twenty-seven men plus the four outside, plus the two in the west wing guarding Pharaoh's harem. A formidable number of nasty-tempered killers.

She swept the binoculars around the room and found the piano in the far right corner. Her breath quickened as she took in the sight of Jordan dressed in formal attire. He looked dashing and handsome and professional, the epitome of a world-class musician. His expression gave nothing away. He looked as if playing for a criminal gang was a perfectly normal event.

Sydney put the binocularss in the small pack on the ground next to her and pulled the short quiver of arrows from it. She unbuckled her belt, slid the quiver onto it, and refastened the buckle.

It was time to get down to business. The Captain was waiting for her to dispatch the guards. She worked her way back to the west wing.

"Stay, Dogma. I'll be back for you, I promise." Sydney set the ironwood staff next to Dogma, pulled the crossbow sling off her shoulder and then stood and climbed over the wall. She crouched in its shadow and waited for the first guard to come toward her.

"Sydney." The whisper came from behind her.

Sydney turned and saw the Captain's head above the wall.

The Captain beckoned her to him. "Do not shoot to kill," he said softly. "Aim for a thigh or shoulder."

Sydney furrowed her brow. "Why? I've been practicing, I can do this."

"I'm sure you can, but I don't want you to. This is not your fight, and I don't want you carrying the burden of murder when this is all done. Incapacitate the guards and we'll take it from there."

"Captain." Sydney's throat worked as she tried to squeeze the words out. "I-I've killed before." She couldn't look at him, couldn't face the look of condemnation she knew she'd see in the Captain's eyes once he knew she was a killer. When he said nothing, she raised her eyes to his.

The Captain reached out a hand and placed it gently on her cheek. "You have a warm and loving soul, Sydney. If you have killed then I know you had a damn good reason for it.

Tonight there is no such reason. We can accomplish our goal without putting you in that position. Aim for a shoulder or thigh, not to kill."

The compassion in the Captain's eyes and voice made Sydney's knees tremble. She pressed his hand to her cheek, then dropped it. "Thank you, Captain. You have no idea how much your words mean to me."

She pressed her back to the wall and waited for the guard to approach. In spite of the seriousness of the situation, relief that she didn't have to kill again made Sydney feel buoyant, almost carefree.

The guard walked the length of the west wing, then leaned against the corner and lit a cigarette. Sydney notched an arrow, took a deep breath, aimed and shot. The arrow hit the guard's thigh with a dull thud. He grunted and fell to the ground.

Two of the Captain's men leaped over the wall, gagged and tied the downed guard and dragged him into the bushes. They relieved him of his weapons, flattened themselves against the house and gave Sydney a thumbs up.

Sydney crouched behind the wall again and made her way to the east wing where she carried out the same exercise. Two more men replaced the guard. She moved to the north side of the house and took out the two guards there, leaving four men in their place, then retrieved Dogma and returned to where the Captain waited.

The remainder of the Captain's ragtag army lay spread out behind the stone wall. Dogma nuzzled Sydney when she rejoined them and licked her face.

Now their plan became an uncertain waiting game. Everything depended on Anna and whether she had added Melody's sedative to the stew. Sydney thought of Anna eating at the table and wondered if the ever-hungry giant had dosed herself.

The low hoo-hoo of a great-horned owl sounded from the rear of the house.

"There's the signal," the Captain said. "It's time to move, folks. Those on my left, stay behind the wall until you reach the corner of the west wing, then run low and fast to the house in case anyone looks out a window. Those on my right, same thing to the east wing. Take care of anyone on the second floor of the wings, then meet up at the main entrance and head straight for the hallway next to the ballroom. Sydney and I will handle the harem guards and meet you there when we can."

Everyone moved off. Sydney heard tools clink and froze, then remembered that Pharaoh's guards were bound and gagged. She peered over the wall and watched the dark shadows, an oddly shaped army with farm tool weapons, move toward the east and west wings.

"Ready? Nock an arrow and follow me." The Captain limped to their left.

Sydney reloaded her pistol. Grabbing Dogma's ruff in her left hand she followed the Captain. He glanced back at the dog, hesitated, but said nothing. They stepped through a gate in the wall and made their way to the rear of the west wing where a series of sliding doors opened onto the long stone patio that ran along the entire back of the house.

The Captain tried two doors, both locked. The third was locked as well. He swore, took off his hat and placed it over his fist, then punched out a pane of glass. He reached through the broken pane and unlocked the door.

Sydney and Dogma followed him inside. There was enough light from the yard lights for Sydney to make out a large bare bed, a dresser, and a stuffed chair. The room appeared to be unused.

The Captain walked to the hallway door and placed his ear against it. "I don't hear anything." He turned the knob slowly and pulled the door open a crack. A slant of dim light from the hallway entered the room.

The Captain opened the door far enough to peer into the hall, then beckoned to Sydney. He turned toward her and put his finger to his lips, cautioning her to be quiet, then pointed to his left.

Sydney nodded her understanding and readied her pistol. She followed the Captain into a wide hallway. Evenly spaced windows filled the wall to their right and faced the front lawn. The bedrooms opened off the hall and faced the rear of the house.

There was no one in the hallway. She wondered where the harem guards were, expecting to see the two men standing at attention outside one of the doors, then realized they would want to be where they could watch the women.

The Captain checked the two bedrooms they had passed and rejoined her. He walked to the next room and pressed his ear to the door, shook his head and moved silently down the hall.

At the next door he stopped and listened again, then nodded at her. They had located Pharaoh's harem. The Captain's jaw tightened, the only outward sign of the cold fury Sydney felt thrumming off him.

Her hands began to sweat and her pulse pounded. She recalled Melody's story about the Captain's wife and daughter. If his daughter were still alive he would find her in this room. Fear pooled in Sydney's stomach. She didn't know if she was strong enough to face whatever lay behind this door.

She thought of Shannon and gathered her courage. She

owed it to her sister to help these girls. She stood against the wall to one side of the door, her pistol raised, gave Dogma the signal to stay, and nodded at the Captain. She was ready.

The Captain grabbed the doorknob and slowly turned it. His body tensed. He flung open the door and darted into the room with Sydney on his tail.

Sydney's eyes darted around the room as she searched for her targets, trying to take it all in. The bedroom was a large room overcrowded with three big beds. Deep pile carpeting felt thick and soft under her feet.

Five or six women lay crowded together on each bed. Two looked at her with deeply shadowed eyes, the rest lay still, staring at nothing, and ignored her.

She spotted a large bald man sitting on the corner of one bed, his sausage-like fingers high on a girl's thigh. He looked at Sydney in surprise and started to pull his hand away. She aimed at his chest, then shot him in the shoulder.

The Captain leaped on the man and twisted his head. The man slumped on the bed and the girl kicked at the body until he slid to the floor. "Where's the other one?" he asked.

One of the shadow-eyed women nodded to a door on their right. "Bathroom."

The raspy whisper of her voice sent a shiver down Sydney's spine.

She nocked another arrow and followed the Captain to the bathroom door. She heard low, steady grunts coming from behind the door and wished she didn't have to see what was on the other side. Something must have shown on her face because the Captain gave her a questioning look. She pressed her lips together, nodded, and he flung open the door.

The second guard lay on top of a young girl, his pants down around his ankles, pressing the girl's naked body into the cold tile floor. Sydney didn't hesitate—she shot the guard in the buttock.

The Captain leaped onto the guard's back and broke his neck, cutting off the guard's howl of pain. He rolled the guard's body off the unconscious girl, then wrapped her naked body in a towel. He gently gathered the girl in his arms and carried her out to the hallway.

Sydney raced ahead of the pair and quietly summoned the four men watching the west wing. The Captain handed the girl through a hallway window with instructions to carry her beyond the wall to the women waiting there. He bade the others to help get the rest of the women and girls out of the house.

Some of the girls, the ones who had been kidnapped elsewhere and brought to Driftwood, were reluctant to go with the Captain's men. While Sydney helped wrap sheets and blankets around their naked bodies she talked quietly with them, asking for their trust, telling them they had nothing to fear from the men.

All the women bore the marks of violence: black eyes, broken noses, swollen jaws, cigarette burn marks, bruises on their arms and legs and buttocks.

One girl in particular seemed to have suffered a great deal of physical abuse. When the Captain took her into his arms and cried Sydney knew it had to be his daughter.

The girl wrapped her arms around the Captain's neck. "I knew you'd come for me, Daddy," she whispered into his neck.

The Captain clung to his daughter, stroking her back and cooing soft words of comfort into her ear. Pain and love showed raw on his face.

Tears sprung to Sydney's eyes as she turned away from the pair. Why couldn't someone have stepped in and saved her sister Shannon? Who decided that these girls deserved to be saved while Shannon did not? A new ball of fury over Shannon's death burned in her chest.

Someone entered the room and reminded the Captain that the others were waiting to begin the assault on the ballroom. He handed his daughter over to the man's waiting arms with obvious reluctance.

When he headed down the hall toward the ballroom, his fierce expression told Sydney that he had set aside John Templeton, loving father, and brought out Captain Templeton, pissed off Marine Corp officer.

25

SYDNEY FOLLOWED the Captain and four others into the entry foyer. The slate-floored foyer filled the entire width of the central portion of the house and soared three stories high. Exposed beams framed the large panes of glass that over-looked the fountain in the center of the circular driveway.

The wooden beams reminded Sydney of her grandfather's barn and she felt a momentary longing to be lying in the warmth of the hayloft, looking out at the Mississippi River while Shannon and her mother worked in the gardens below.

She shook off her nostalgia and craned her neck to gape at the massive wrought iron chandelier that hung from the roof to the second floor from a long black chain.

A wide, split staircase went up each side of the foyer and created a landing on the second level. The ballroom doors opened onto the landing.

Male voices and piano notes bounced around the foyer as the Captain led them under the landing and through a door into the east wing. The east wing was a mirror image of the west wing, with a wide hallway and rooms that opened off the hall toward the rear of the house.

The Captain opened the first door and Sydney saw that it contained a staircase, not the bedroom she had expected. She followed the others up the stairs and found herself in another hallway identical to the one below.

A set of double doors separated the hall from the second floor landing. The noise from the ballroom sounded much louder here. The Captain knocked briefly on the first bedroom door. It opened, revealing a room full of grim-faced farmers.

"Did you get them?" asked one of the women.

"Yes," answered the Captain. "We cleaned out the harem—seventeen in all. They're safely away from the house and being looked after. We're ready to take on Pharaoh and the rest of his men. Nine of Pharaoh's guards are either dead or incapacitated. That leaves twenty-eight men."

Sydney felt some of the tension seep out of the room at the news of the girls' safety. Now the odds were in the farmer's favor—there were no hostages to tie their hands.

"There's no telling if the sedative has worked; we'll have to assume that it hasn't and hit them hard and ferocious. Make no noise until the battle has engaged."

The Captain looked over their faces and nodded with satisfaction at what he saw in them. He turned to Sydney. "I want you and Dogma to take care of Jordan. Leave Pharaoh and his men to us. Get the piano player clear of the house and wait for us outside."

Sydney started to protest but held her tongue. The Captain was right, Jordan was her priority. She had already helped to disarm almost one-fourth of Pharaoh's men. The others could finish the job without her.

She nodded her agreement and the Captain gave her a quick smile that transformed his face. For a brief moment she saw the man he must have been before the women he loved were taken from him.

Everyone filed from the bedroom in silence and gathered at the double doors, with Sydney and Dogma at the rear. Her plan was to slide in after the initial attack and while everyone was occupied lead Jordan out of the house.

She notched an arrow just in case something went awry, and hefted her grandfather's staff in her left hand. Dogma pressed to her side, tensed and ready for action. Sydney pressed back against the huge dog, grateful for her presence.

The Captain raised his fist in the air and the double doors quietly opened. The farmers flowed through them: a lethal, angry army ready to take back what was theirs.

Sydney's pulse quickened as she stepped through the doors onto the landing and waited for the confrontation to begin.

It took several moments for the occupants of the ballroom to realize they were under attack. The conversations stopped abruptly. Shouts of disbelief and surprise were joined by the battle cries of the angry farmers.

Farm implements swung. Men fell. Pharaoh's men were slow to react, unsteady on their feet. Sydney let out her breath in a relieved sigh; Anna had put the sedative in the stew after all.

She skirted around the edge of the ballroom toward the left corner where Jordan sat at the piano, head cocked, eyes wide.

Out of the corner of her eye she saw Sandman wrap his arms around a woman and force a shovel from her hand. Sydney shouted for someone to come to the woman's aid, but no one was free to help. She knew she had only moments before Sandman broke the woman's neck.

Sydney ran forward toward the pair. When Sandman released one arm and raised it to grasp the woman's head she stopped to take a steady aim. Her arrow lodged in Sandman's buttock.

He howled and whirled toward Sydney, letting go of his captive. She scrambled free, picked up her shovel, and whacked Sandman in the back of his head. He fell to the floor and stayed there. The woman grinned at Sydney, hog-tied her prisoner, and headed back into the fray.

Sydney recovered the dropped staff and made it to the grand piano without further incident. "Jordan! It's Sydney and Dogma. Are you all right? We need to get you out of here."

Jordan smiled at her. He looked remarkably calm in spite of the chaos around him.

"I knew it was you, you didn't have to tell me. I'd know your scent and voice anywhere. It sounds as though you have the entire town with you. I heard you shoot someone a minute ago."

"I shot Sandman before he could kill again. He's now trussed up and out of action."

Jordan reached out a hand.

Sydney grabbed it and squeezed. "Most of the town is here. After Pharaoh's men took you away the farmers decided they'd had enough. I'll tell you all about it later. Right now we have to get out of the house. Here, take my grandfather's staff." She pulled her hand free and replaced it with the ironwood staff.

Jordan grabbed the staff and ran his hand over the ram's head. "Thank you, I've missed this." He stood and closed the piano lid to protect the keyboard, then stepped away from the piano.

Dogma launched herself at him, set her front paws on Jordan's shoulders, and licked his face. He laughed and rubbed her head. "I'm glad to see you too, Dogma."

Sydney looked around the ballroom. "Is there a back way out of here? It's crowded over by the main doors."

Jordan nodded as he lowered Dogma to the floor. "There's a back stair that leads to the kitchen. Apparently the original owner had it built to keep the kitchen help out of the way when they served at his parties. It's located on the opposite corner from the piano. I hear Pharaoh's servants coming and going from there while I play."

Sydney nocked her last arrow and took Jordan's hand.

He entwined his fingers through hers and squeezed. "I wondered if I'd ever hold your hand like this again," he said, his voice raw. "I was afraid I'd never see you again."

Sydney didn't answer; she couldn't speak around the lump in her throat. Someday maybe she'd tell Jordan how much he meant to her, but now wasn't the time.

She squeezed his fingers instead and pulled him toward kitchen stairs. She opened the door and ushered Jordan through it, then turned back to the room to check on the battle.

Her team was winning. Most of Pharaoh's men lay trussed like calves on the floor. The farmers must have all carried rope with them for just that reason, mused Sydney.

She followed Jordan through the door and stopped to listen. They were alone in the stairwell. The wide staircase had been built to accommodate multiple people carrying large, heavy trays. Light from the yard filtered in through a tall window that ran from the kitchen level to the second story.

The battle behind them grew quieter. No sound rose from the kitchen below.

They walked three abreast down the stairs. Jordan used the staff to feel the steps as they descended, his other hand wound in Dogma's ruff. If a dog could smile, then Dogma grinned with happiness at having Jordan back.

Sydney knew just how she felt. She had a grin on her face as well.

They stopped at the closed door at the bottom and listened again. Still no sound from the kitchen.

"Have you been in the kitchen?" whispered Sydney.

Jordan shook his head in a silent no.

Sydney recalled what she had seen of the kitchen earlier and oriented their position with her mental image. If she remembered right, they should enter the kitchen near the windows at the back of the house, close to an exit door. That was good, they might be able to sneak out of the kitchen without being seen.

"Wait here." She slowly cracked the door open and peered into the large space. She could only see the wall of windows and parts of stainless work tables. The sinks and cabinets and table where Anna had sat eating were behind the door. She still heard no sound.

Sydney took a deep breath and pushed the door open wider. Behind her, Dogma growled. She tried to pull the door closed again but the knob was yanked out of her hand. The door slammed open against the wall with a bang that made her jump.

A short, skinny man stood there, a gun in his raised hand. His tattooed, bald head glistened under the kitchen lights. Pale, icy blue eyes glittered at Sydney with cold intelligence.

"Well, well, who do we have here? Aren't you going to introduce me to your beautiful friend, Jordan?"

The man's voice sounded surprisingly deep coming from his skinny chest. Sydney couldn't move. Her feet and legs felt like limestone blocks. Her hand trembled as she held the crossbow down by her leg and slightly behind her. She felt Jordan stiffen beside her.

"Pharaoh, this is my very good friend Sydney. Sydney, meet Pharaoh." Jordan's voice betrayed none of the tension he felt.

Shock passed through Sydney's body. This scrawny man had terrorized the town of Driftwood? She wondered where he had found the gun. It occurred to her that Pharaoh could be bluffing—the gun might not be loaded.

Pharaoh reached out his free hand and motioned to Sydney. "You're coming with me. Something tells me I've outlived my welcome in this town. It's time to move on to new pastures. You can keep me entertained on the way."

Sydney didn't move. She heard Jordan draw a ragged breath. Dogma growled low in her throat.

Pharaoh jerked when he heard Dogma. He stepped closer to the doorway and saw her behind Jordan. His face paled. "I hate dogs. Where did that beast come from?"

"She belongs to me," answered Jordan. "What are you doing in the kitchen, Pharaoh? Why aren't you with your men?"

"I knew something was wrong. I never eat with my men. My meals are specially prepared from the best ingredients. The men get more common fare. When they began to act dopey I decided to check with the kitchen staff. Imagine my surprise to find them all fast asleep."

Pharaoh pointed the gun at Dogma. "I told you to come stand by me," he said, looking at Sydney. "I assure you, this gun is loaded. Turns out the previous owner was a gun nut and believed in keeping a plentiful supply of ammo on hand.

I'll count to three. If you aren't standing by my side I'll shoot the dog first, then the piano player. One."

Sydney looked into Pharaoh's cold eyes and knew if she refused he would kill Dogma and Jordan. She took a step forward.

Pharaoh gave her an evil grin. His eyes raked her body in a way that made her skin crawl with disgust and loathing.

He spotted her crossbow and his eyes narrowed. "Drop the weapon. Don't even think of trying to use it. I can shoot faster than you can lift and aim, and I promise I'll catch your boyfriend right in the throat. Two."

Sydney's hands trembled. The urge to shoot the hateful monster standing before her threatened to overwhelm her. She forced herself to drop the crossbow and kicked it back toward Jordan to keep it out of Pharaoh's hands.

"Good. I like an obedient woman. Now step over here. Three."

"Sydney, no." Jordan reached out and grabbed a handful of Sydney's shirt.

"I have to, Jordan. Let me go." Sydney took two steps farther into the kitchen and looked for the kitchen workers. She saw Anna slumped over a picnic table with two short, round women dressed in white coats opposite her. Gentle snores told her they were still alive.

Behind her Jordan and Dogma stood silent. She could feel their tension and knew they were waiting for an opportunity to help her.

Pharaoh reached out and slapped her face, snapping her head to one side. "That's for kicking the weapon away."

Sydney blinked back tears from the unexpected slap. She stared at the tiled floor, her cheek burning. Her eyes followed the black and white pattern while she tried to think of what to do. Fear for Jordan and Dogma clouded her thoughts.

Suddenly a memory filled her mind, clear and sharp as if it was happening right then. She had been upset about something that day, railing against the world, destroying innocent plants and throwing rocks, taking out her anger on whatever entered her path.

Smokey was with her. He ignored her, which had pissed her off even more. He continued to ignore her until they stood together on a bluff top high above the shining Mississippi.

"Sydney." Smokey broke the silence after allowing her to fume for several more minutes. "Events happen, we meet people, we see and experience places—that's what life is made of. All those things are important, but in the end, it is our thoughts about them that matter most."

Sydney stared at him, still angry, but trying to understand what he was telling her. Smokey always had a message in his words.

"Life brings us the people, places, and events we need to grow. We change the world around us by changing our thoughts about these things. Sometimes we do it by letting go. Sometimes we open up and gain a little more understanding and that changes our perspective. It's all part of being human, this capacity to think, to understand, and to change."

It had taken Sydney a while to understand Smokey's message. She had examined her anger on that day and discovered a truth about herself. She could choose to indulge in anger, or she could do something about it.

Just as the anger had drained away that day, Sydney's fear drained away now. She was no longer the terrified young woman who lay hidden in the hayloft while her sister was raped and murdered.

Yes, she had killed two men and killing was wrong. But perhaps there were times when it was justified. She looked at Pharaoh and knew in her heart that some men were simply too evil to be allowed to live, too evil to be allowed to wreak their havoc upon the innocent.

Sydney turned her head and looked at Jordan and Dogma standing in the doorway, waiting to help her. She knew Pharaoh would not let them live. She felt her love for them fill her heart.

She could not let them die.

Karma made allowances for the victims of evil, she felt sure of it. More important, it made allowances for those who were forced to kill the evil doers.

She looked at Pharaoh and smiled. She had nothing to lose. "I'm not going anywhere with you. Sorry." Sydney flung herself against Pharaoh's gun arm and stuck out her foot to trip him.

The unexpected attack and Pharaoh's small size worked in her favor. He stumbled back a couple steps and caught up against a work table.

Dogma snarled and leaped at Pharaoh, fangs bared, and knocked him to the floor. The gun skidded under the table as he threw up his arms to protect himself. Dogma stood over him, her teeth bared near his throat, daring him to move.

Her low growl raised the hair on the back of Sydney's neck.

"Call off your dog. I'll let you go, I promise." Pharaoh's eyes were wide with terror, his face a deathly white.

Sydney picked up her crossbow. She located the fallen arrow and nocked it, then returned to Pharaoh.

"The thing is, you really don't mean it," she said thought-fully. "You are far too evil to set free."

She aimed the crossbow at Pharaoh's chest. "This is for all the women you've raped and killed, and for my sister Shannon."

"Sydney, wait." Jordan made his way to where she stood. He felt for her shoulder and ran his hand down her arm until he covered her trigger finger with his own.

"We do this together," he said. "Now."

Together they sent the arrow through Pharaoh's heart.

26

JORDAN PULLED Sydney to his chest and wrapped his arms around her. "You okay?"

Sydney sagged against him, her knees suddenly weak. The feel of Jordan's firm body and muscled arms felt reassuring and safe. She turned her face into his chest and nodded. "I'm okay. Pharaoh needed to die and I was elected."

She pulled her head away from Jordan's chest and looked up at him. It was time to come clean. To confess what a terrible person she really was.

"Pharaoh isn't the first man I've killed," she said carefully. "After Shannon was raped and murdered two men found me. I knew the same fate awaited me. I pushed one to his death and killed the second man with a frying pan after he killed my grandfather."

Jordan rubbed his large hands over Sydney's back. "I'm so sorry. You didn't deserve to go through a horrible experience like that."

Jordan's hands felt comforting like her father's used to be whenever she was ill or upset.

"You're wrong—I did need to go through that," she said. "I

hated myself for allowing Shannon to die. And I hated myself for being no better than the man who killed my sister. I hated myself for being a murderer. I thought that I deserved to suffer for the rest of my life."

She looked down at the body at their feet. "Tonight, after seeing what these men have done to innocent men, women, and children, my thinking changed. I understand now that evil is real, and what is more important, I understand that it's necessary to defend against it. I did the right thing, then and now, and I can live with that."

Jordan lifted her chin with one hand and pulled her closer with the other arm. He bent his head to hers and gave her a soft kiss. "You are an amazing woman, Sydney Waters." He kissed her again, harder this time.

Sydney wrapped her arms around Jordan's neck and kissed him back with all the fiery passion she had inherited from her Italian mother. She pressed her body against his, needing to get closer.

Jordan groaned and slid one hand to her bottom and pulled her tight against him. "You're making me crazy, Syd," he whispered as he planted kisses down her throat.

A loud snore broke through Sydney's fogged senses and she pulled away from Jordan. What was she thinking? Losing her virginity while standing in a kitchen with three sleeping cooks and a dead body was not how she wanted her first time to be.

"We have to stop," she rasped. "This isn't right."

"It felt right to me," said Jordan, "but I see your point." He loosened his hold on her. His gray eyes were still smoky with passion. "These aren't exactly the surroundings a man wants to make love to his girl in, especially the first time."

Jordan ran a finger along Sydney's jaw. "To be continued at another time." He bent his head and kissed her gently. "Definitely to be continued," he said against her mouth.

Sydney spent the next two weeks at the Leighton mansion helping the families of Driftwood put their lives back together.

There were several arguments about what to do with the convicts. Some people wanted to execute them, others wanted to chain them in the barn where their children were held prisoner and starve them. In the end they decided to return them to the Penton penitentiary and feed them gruel for the rest of their lives.

Melody felt that several of the children were too weak and ill to move, and she wanted to keep her eye on everyone until they showed signs of improvement. The mansion had power and hot water, plus keeping her patients all in one place made the doc's life easier.

The parents took turns tending their farms and sitting with their offspring. Understandably, no parent wanted any child left alone.

On the rare occasion that both parents were away, Sydney sat with the child and told stories while they waited for a parent to return. She loved the one-on-one time with the kids. Their resiliency amazed and humbled her.

She grew fond of one young boy in particular. While many of the children continued to feel fearful and had nightmares, Althea's nine-year old son Amos maintained his irrepressible good humor. Amos had single-handedly kept up the other's spirits with his lively wit and storytelling abilities while held captive in the dairy barn.

Sydney made a point to stop by Amos's room every day. He made her laugh and helped restore her own spirit.

Her life at the mansion quickly settled into a regular routine. When she wasn't entertaining a child, she stripped and changed beds, washed laundry, helped prepare food, and carried meals to the rooms of the kids still too weak to sit in the ballroom.

The children who had recovered enough strength to walk to the ballroom were entertained by Jordan and Dogma. Jordan dressed in his tuxedo and played children's standards, made up silly songs about individuals—including their parents, which often brought gales of laughter from everyone.

The kids loved Jordan's giant dog and Dogma enjoyed the attention they lavished upon her. The ballroom became the social center of the mansion, with plenty of room for those who had regained their strength to run and play ball and act like normal children.

Sydney's only worry was the girls rescued from Pharaoh's harem. They were not bouncing back as readily as the kids. Although well enough to take their meals in the ballroom, they sat somewhat apart from the others and spoke very little beyond polite, shallow conversation. Mostly they sat and watched the children with shuttered expressions.

Sydney knew the trauma these girls suffered was harder to repair. She began to sit with them at every opportunity, looking for a way to acknowledge their pain and bring it out into the open, to put a stop to the festering wounds.

One morning, two weeks after Pharaoh's downfall, she found herself sitting at a table with the Captain's daughter, Karen. Karen's bruises had faded to a sickly yellow and the swelling on her face had receded enough for her to eat normal food.

This morning Karen merely played with her food, cutting a piece of french toast into little bits and pushing the pieces around her plate.

Sydney watched Karen for several minutes while she ate her own breakfast. She had a feeling she knew what was eating at the teenager. She knew she should wait for Karen to bring it up, but the urge to help the girl made her impatient. "It's not your fault, you know."

Karen looked up from her plate with a startled expression. "What are you talking about?"

"It's not your fault that Pharaoh's men killed your mother."

Karen narrowed her eyes at Sydney. "How do you know? You weren't there."

Sydney heard the anger and despair in Karen's voice and knew she had guessed right. "I can see that something's eating at you. Based on my recent experiences, I have an idea that you're feeling guilty."

"You don't know anything. It's my fault my mother is dead and Dad has a bum leg. They didn't want to come into Driftwood that afternoon, but I whined and nagged until they gave in. So you see, it is my fault."

Sydney nodded and leaned closer to Karen. "Yeah, I felt the same way when I watched from the safety of my grandfather's hayloft as three men raped and killed my sister. It was my fault Shannon died because I didn't help her."

Karen's eyes widened. She set down her fork and clenched her hands in her lap. "How-how do you live with that guilt? I feel this big, black space inside and it's tearing me up." Her slim throat convulsed. "I want to die too," she whispered.

Sydney reached out and covered Karen's hands. "I finally realized that I did the best I could at the time. There's also this thing called karma. Have you ever heard of it? It's one of the cornerstones of life. I can best describe it as, what goes around comes around."

Sydney inched her chair closer to Karen and lowered her voice. "I've learned some things recently. There is real evil in the world, and sometimes innocent people get touched by that evil and we can't do anything to stop it."

Karen's shoulders sagged but she didn't pull her hand away. Her eyes shone with tears. "If it wasn't for me, the evil wouldn't have touched my mom."

"That's not true. We have no control over when or if evil shows up. You didn't do anything wrong. Your mother's death was out of your hands. If it didn't happen on that day it would've caught her on another."

Sydney groped for a way to explain. "Your mother didn't deserve to be touched by evil that day, but it found her. Karma works over a long period, not just in this lifetime. The good news is that karma has a partner, known as grace. Grace will compensate your mother for the evil she suffered in a very special and generous way, perhaps in her next life. You may even be there to be a part of it."

A glimmer of hope showed in Karen's eyes. She dashed the tears away with her free hand. "Karma and grace. My mother would have liked the symmetry of that."

Karen gently pulled away from Sydney's grasp and picked up her fork. She put a bit of the french toast in her mouth and chewed slowly, thinking. "I need to tell Dad about grace. I know he feels even worse about Mom than I do. Thanks, Sydney."

Sydney stood and squeezed Karen's shoulder. "You're very welcome. If you come across anyone else having guilt issues about something they have no control over, be sure to share it."

She checked on a couple children, then noticed Jordan sitting alone at the piano. She had avoided being alone with him after their passionate scene in the kitchen. Jordan was an experienced man of the world, while she was little more than a country bumpkin. Now that Jordan had had time to reconsider their kiss she felt sure he regretted it.

Her breath caught in her chest. She couldn't leave Driftwood without saying goodbye. They were still friends weren't they? She hesitated, then squared her shoulders and made her way across the room.

Jordan sensed her presence before she spoke. He would always know when she was near.

He plastered a smile on his face to hide his anxiety. Sydney had avoided him since he had kissed her. She obviously had thought things over and decided the kiss had been a mistake. Somehow he needed to convince her that they belonged together.

"Good morning, Sydney." He made an effort to keep his voice light and friendly. "I haven't seen much of you lately. Been busy?" He patted the bench next to him. "Sit with me for a minute, I've missed your company."

Sydney scooted onto the piano bench, careful to leave a few inches of space between them. Even though they weren't touching, she was aware of the heat of his body and flushed at the memory of how good it had felt pressed against hers.

"I've been trying to make myself useful." She caught the slight strain in her voice and took a deep breath. "Things are starting to quiet down now, though. Most of the kids from the barn bounced back remarkably fast. They seem to love your music by the way."

Jordan's grin lit his whole face. "It's fun to play for them. They're an appreciative audience, something every performer loves."

Sydney watched Jordan's long, strong fingers float over the piano keys. She examined his profile, committing it to memory: strong jaw, full lips, strong, straight nose, and gray eyes that changed from warm and smoky to icy steel depending on his mood.

She didn't ever want to forget Jordan's face. He meant more to her than anyone alive. Leaving him behind would be difficult, but it was necessary. She had to be strong and do the right thing. Traveling was too dangerous for a blind man. Here the people of Driftwood could care for him and keep him safe.

She took another deep breath, let it out. "I think it's time for me to leave. I need to get back on the road. Althea offered me some of her dried jerky. I wondered if you'd let me take the two hens with me for eggs. I promise to take good care of them." Her throat choked up tight and she blinked back sudden tears. This was more difficult than she imagined.

Jordan's fingers stilled upon the keyboard. "You're leaving? So soon? Do you have to go? I hoped we could share a house or an apartment here, provided we could find one. We could make a place for ourselves in Driftwood."

Jordan felt as if his heart had stopped beating. He couldn't bear the thought of Sydney leaving. Even though they hadn't talked much over the last two weeks his thoughts had been filled with her. She had become the most important person in his life.

He breathed in the scent that was unique to Sydney and tried to imagine his life without her in it. It stretched bleak and empty, into a dark and lonely future.

Sydney placed her hand on Jordan's thigh and felt it tense. She hastily moved her hand and dropped it into her own lap. "If I was going to set up house with anyone, I would choose you, Jordan. You are the closest friend I have and I hate the thought of leaving you."

"Then why are you going? That makes no sense. Stay here with me. Please, Sydney."

"I can't stay. It's hard to explain, but something is pushing me to find Smokey. Perhaps after I find him I can come back to Driftwood and join you. If you haven't found someone else by then, that is."

She tried to make light of it, but Sydney's gut twisted at the thought of another woman caring for Jordan. She knew that several of Driftwood's single women found him attractive and flirted with him at every opportunity.

She took another deep breath and searched for the words to explain her need to leave. "Right now I feel as if there's something driving me, something unfinished that I'm supposed to do. I won't be able to settle anywhere until I understand what it is."

Sydney stood up and brushed her lips lightly over Jordan's. She wanted to sink into his lap and put her arms around him, wanted to hold him close and feel him respond to her. She forced herself to straighten and stepped back from the bench.

"You'll be safe here and that's important to me, Jordan. Besides, we're opposites—you're a man of the world and I'm just a simple country girl. You can do better than me, you'll see. I won't ever forget you."

She bent down and gave Dogma a hug, burying her face in the beast's fur for a moment. "Bye, Dogma. You're the most awesome dog I've ever known."

She straightened and hurried away before Jordan could say anything to make her change her mind. She had one last person to see. Sydney made her way down to the kitchen where Anna stood over the stove.

"Anna! I wanted to say good-bye and wish you well."

Over the last two weeks Sydney had watched Anna change. She no longer begged constantly for food. Melody had taken her on as an assistant and was training her to help care for the sick animals. She also helped cook the evening meal at the Leighton mansion, which had been turned into a hospice/orphanage. Regular meals and gainful employment had done wonders for Anna's disposition.

Anna turned from the stove and smiled at Sydney. "Are you hungry?"

Sydney laughed and shook her head. "No, I've eaten, thank you. I just wanted to let you know I'm leaving in the morning. I hope to return to Driftwood sometime, but if I don't, I wanted you to know that I'm proud of you, and I'm glad you've found a place for yourself."

To Sydney's surprise, Anna reached out and patted her shoulder, then returned her attention to the pots on the stoves. "Maybe you'll find a place too."

Sydney smiled and took her leave.

27

THE FOLLOWING morning dawned with a thin, gray overcast that matched Sydney's gloomy mood. She lay in her bed and wondered if she really wanted to leave Driftwood. It would be so much easier to stay. She had made friends here; good people like Melody and the Captain, people she regretted leaving behind. She knew she could make a place for herself in Driftwood. She could rent an apartment with Jordan and help him find his place in the new world.

No. Despite her words to the Captain's daughter Karen, Sydney still blamed herself for Shannon's death. She needed to resume her journey, needed to find her friend Smokey. Smokey was the only one still alive who understood how important Shannon had been to her. He was the only one who could help her heal after her loss.

Mind made up, Sydney quickly dressed. She ate a last hot breakfast of oatmeal, donned her pack, and managed to sneak out of the mansion without seeing Jordan. She headed south on the main drag out of town. Once clear of Driftwood she planned to cut over to a gravel road and resume traveling the lesser used roads.

As the sun climbed higher, a light breeze picked up and blew apart the gray clouds. The gloomy morning turned bright and sunny. Sydney picked up her pace, glad to be moving again after being in one place for so long.

She walked steadily for an hour, her mind purposely blank. Thinking would bring the memory of the look on Jordan's face when she kissed him goodbye. She thought she detected hunger and determination in his eyes when she turned to leave.

Just wishful thinking, she told herself. Stop thinking about Jordan. He's better off staying with people who can look after him. It won't be long before another girl catches his attention.

The thought depressed her.

She placed one foot in front of the other, eyes on the road, and ignored the pain in her heart. She hoped that distance would eventually ease her pain, but this morning each step away from Driftwood and the man she loved only made the hurt grow stronger.

Sydney crested a small rise and looked out to the road ahead. Her heart stuttered. A solitary man walked a quarter mile in front her.

A man with a giant dog at his side.

A man wearing a backpack and carrying a carved staff.

As she drew near, the man stopped and turned toward her.

"Well, you coming or not?" asked Jordan. "I was beginning to worry that I'd picked the wrong road." His face split into a broad smile. "Surprise. You didn't think I was going to stay put and miss out on the greatest adventure of my life, did you?"

Sydney thought her heart was going to leap out of her

chest. She ran forward. The chickens squawked in protest as their cages bounced against her pack.

She slipped out of her pack and flung herself at Jordan. "What are you doing here?" she asked. She was shaking, she felt so happy to see him. She wrapped her arms tight around Jordan's waist and pressed her face into his chest.

When Jordan didn't immediately respond, she disengaged her arms and stepped back in sudden embarrassment.

"Where's Kria?" She was pleased to note that her voice didn't betray her hurt. How could she have been so wrong about Jordan? She had hoped that he had the same feelings for her as she did for him.

She had dared to hope that he loved her. Or at least had grown very, very fond of her.

"It's not safe for her on the road so I left her with Doc Melody," answered Jordan. "Kria has animal companions at Melody's place and plenty to eat. She'll be happy and well cared for there. Melody plans to use her as a therapy pony for the kids."

Jordan dropped his staff and reached out for Sydney. He caught the edge of her sleeve and pulled her closer, running his hands up her arms to grip her shoulders. He cupped her face between his hands.

"You took me by surprise. I didn't know if you'd be happy to see me again," he murmured as he brought his lips down on hers.

He kissed her gently at first, his lips tender against hers. Then he wrapped his arms around her and pulled her tight against his body and his lips demanded more from her.

As Jordan persisted and deepened his kiss Sydney's fears and worries melted under the intensity of her desire for him.

When Jordan finally broke away, his gray eyes glittered like molten silver. "What was that crap you tried to give me yesterday about you being country and me being city? Haven't you ever heard that opposites attract?"

He didn't give her a chance to answer. "We're good together. I want to be a part of your life." His eyes looked into hers and Sydney felt as if he saw into her soul.

"Tell me you'll let us join you, Sydney. Dogma was heartbroken when you left her behind."

Sydney felt giddy and weak-kneed with happiness. She dug her fingers into Jordan's thick hair and brought his face down to hers.

"Well, I certainly can't hurt Dogma's feelings, can I?" she whispered, then kissed him again.

I'm glad you found this book out of the millions available. If you'd like to know what else I've written or when I release a new book instead of leaving it to chance, you can sign up for my newsletter or send me an email through my website CharleyMarshBooks.com. I love to hear from my readers.

And if you want to know what I'm up to on a more regular basis you can follow me on my website or Facebook. https://www.facebook.com/charley.marsh.372

ABOUT THE AUTHOR

In my younger days my curiosity drove me to climb mountains, canoe rivers, and explore caves and wilderness areas from Maine to California. I've been shot at, caught in a desert flash flood, and almost drowned off the Maine coast. Once I tobogganed down a 5,000+ foot mountain.

Life is always an adventure if you have the right attitude.

I never set out to be a storyteller, but looking back on the elaborate lies I made up as a troubled teen I can see that I always had the makings. Now, in the immortal words of Lawrence Block, I happily "make up lies for fun and profit."